MORTAL
GODS

MORTAL GODS

a novel by

JONATHAN FAST

HARPER & ROW, PUBLISHERS
New York, Hagerstown, San Francisco, London

For Howard and Bette Fast

Acknowledgments

Much of the material dealing with genetics in this novel was drawn from *Genetic Revolution,* by D. S. Halacy, Jr., *The Biological Time Bomb,* by Gordon Rattray Taylor, and Isaac Asimov's excellent book *The Genetic Code.*

The use of fluorocarbons as blood substitutes is drawn loosely from the work of Dr. Leland C. Clark, Jr. My MHD flying saucers were designed by Dr. Richard J. Rosa, and appear in a back issue of *Analog.* Primordial black holes, my ultimate weapon, really do explode with the force of 10 million one-megaton hydrogen bombs—or more! See *The Quantum Mechanics of Black Holes,* by S. W. Hawking, *Scientific American,* Jan. 1977.

Special thanks to Leslie Leinwand of Rockefeller University for her valuable suggestions and corrections.

And thanks to Michael Seidman, Olga Vezeris, Elisabeth Jakab and Sheila Gilbert for editorial advice, Grace Griffin for her encouragement and guidance, Frederick Pohl for a neat detail of the plot, and Erica, as always, for everything.

Now I shall tell of things that change, new being
Out of old . . .

—Ovid, *The Metamorphoses*

PART I
A Distinguished Emissary from Alta-Ty

✿ I ✿

Nick Harmon ascended Post 14 to Morgan Grim's office wondering if this time he was going to be fired. He had fouled up occasionally during his three years in the Public Relations Department at Mutagen Laboratories, but yesterday had been the worst.

A technical paper had been delivered to his robo-sec describing a revolutionary breakthrough in "random mutation prediction." Nick's responsibility was to rewrite it, making it intelligible to the general public, and to distribute it to the news magasettes and holovision stations throughout the Federation of Worlds.

The problem was that Nick hadn't come to work at all that day. Breakfasting at the club he had run into Althea Clinger, an old girl friend of his, and at her suggestion they had visited one of the islands in the sky, an isolated place of sleepy lagoons and rainbow-plumed peacocks. There they had fucked all day and bathed under waterfalls and dozed on mosses, soft as down.

Nick Harmon had a weakness for women, and they generally had a hard time keeping their hands off him. He was twenty-eight, rangy and handsome, with a head of black hair that wouldn't stay combed and a sweet, lopsided grin. His legs were muscular in striped tights, his shoulders broad beneath a turquoise cape. The plain leather codpiece he affected was the latest fashion among young Averyville bachelors.

Arriving at Gamma level disc, Nick hopped out of the post and strode down the corridor to Morgan Grim's office. He ran through a series of excuses, weighing them one by one, wondering which Morgan would be most likely to accept. Sick relative? No. Sick himself? Possibly. Sprained his ankle? Nick tried limping the next few steps. Better, but it still wouldn't explain why he hadn't called in. Had to be something more serious. A MagLev cab accident on the way to work. Pinned beneath a steering fin, hours to clear away the wreckage, miraculously not a scratch on him.

Ridiculous.

3

He reached Morgan's door and slipped his badge in the slot; instantly the door slid open and he stepped inside.

Morgan's robo-sec, a big silver pear, turned on her swivel base to face him.

"Good morning, Nicholas, go right in."

In an attempt to humanize her, someone—certainly not Morgan—had inked in a face where hers should have been: long eyelashes, thick lips. Even a beauty mark.

"You look sensational," Nick said.

"Could you please rephrase the statement?"

Nick laughed and went inside.

Morgan was sitting at his desk, a big palette-shaped slab of lucite, with a holocube in front of him, having an argument with the pygmy head inside the cube. He broke off long enough to wave Nick to a chair, then resumed the exchange.

"We *can't* persuade the Lifestylers to endorse Johnny Quog. Sure, Mutagen creates them, but once they leave our labs they're independent agents and *nobody* tells them what to do. I wouldn't dream of trying. I just control the largest public relations department on the planet. They control the hearts and minds of the whole damn galaxy!"

"Couldn't you call some of them up," the pygmy head pleaded, "and see how they feel? They must favor one of the candidates."

"Look," Morgan said, getting fed up, "never in history has a Lifestyler endorsed a candidate for Federation presidency, and I don't think they're going to start now. But if you're that stuck on the idea you can call them yourself. Goodbye!"

He brought his fist down on the call button and the pygmy head turned gray and vanished; he leaned back in his chair, sighed and stretched, then smiled at Nick.

"How goes it?"

"No complaints," Nick said.

"Isn't that too much? They want me to get a Lifestyler to endorse Johnny Quog. They're busting my balls. But I told them where to get off."

Morgan was in his middle fifties, short and stout, oatmealy skin with a patina of freckles, watery blue eyes, red hair cut so short it bristled. He wore a conservative business cape and tights, and shoes with long curly toes.

"Think they'll win the election?" Nick said absently. In his mind he was still trying to manufacture a plausible excuse for yesterday. Ah, yesterday. Lying on the moss with Althea, her clever tongue exploring his ear, her thighs opening like the gates to heaven. . . .

". . . this Alta-Tyberian thing?"

"Huh?" Nick said, jolted back from his reverie.

"Nicky, for Christ's sake pay attention! Now, how much do you know about the Alta-Tyberians?"

"About as much as the next guy," Nick bluffed. Clearly the presidential elections had been left behind and a new topic introduced. Alta-Tyberians? It did stir a memory.

"Well, none of us knows very much. They're an extremely insular people, almost no contact with the rest of the galaxy. About a thousand years ago they had a fabulous technology—at least that's what I've read. Then they melted down all their machines and became farmers. For fun, I gather, they stand on one foot and stare off into space.

"Physically they're humanoid, but long and skinny like they'd been stretched. Blue skin. The males have a cottony white fur all over their bodies, females just have it on their heads. Some other minor differences in digestive and reproductive apparatus, and possibly psi powers.

"The 2201 star probe was the first to contact them. The Federation offered them a protectorate, but they chose to remain neutral. Then the People's Planetary Alliance offered them worldhood. Federation countered with worldhood plus most-favored-planet status. The Alta-Tys declined everybody, but they've maintained peaceful diplomatic relations."

"Why are they so popular?"

"I'll get to that. Three years ago, early in 2223, a comet tail swept the planet. The radiation caused widespread mutation. Eighty-seven percent of the infants born since have been the Alta-Ty equivalent of Mongoloids. In less than fifty years the entire civilization will be extinct unless—"

"Unless Mutagen can manufacture a replicon. What is it?" Nick continued, getting interested. "A trisomy? A point mutation?"

Morgan shrugged. "Nobody knows. They don't even know their karyotype. But an emissary's scheduled to arrive within the next few weeks with a case of samples."

"We analyze their DNA and create a replicon. That's a lot of work. It took the human race five hundred years, if you start with Mendel."

"It should take us five weeks. During that time the Alta-Ty

emissary is going to be our guest and *you're* going to entertain him."

"I'm honored," Nick said.

"Don't be. You're the only one we can spare for that long."

"And what will I do with this furry fellow?"

"Do whatever you want. Teach him rocket polo. Take him flying. Show him the Lifestyler Temples—every tourist loves that."

"Good idea," Nick agreed. He'd enjoy it himself.

Such were the ironies of fate: here he had come expecting to be fired and instead he was being given what amounted to a five-week vacation with pay. What a pleasure it would be, as long as the Alta-Tyberian wasn't too much bother. *Alta-Tyberians*. Where had he heard of them? Something important. A memory stirred, a magasette article he had read. . . .

"Of course," Nick said, bouncing upright. "That's where the pallinite comes from."

Morgan nodded. "The secret of galactic popularity. Live on a planet that's rich in the one mineral you need for total military superiority."

"They use it in bombs, don't they?"

"Not exactly. If you drain a primordial black hole of antiparticles it collapses like the biggest bomb anybody ever dreamed of. Might have been the nature of the original Big Bang, in fact. But exploding the holes is useless unless you can move them into the right position, and for that you need a tractor beam, and to build a tractor beam you need pallinite. Lots of it."

"We save their civilization, they reciprocate by joining the Federation . . ." Nick's mouth fell open as he realized the implications. "Holy shit."

Morgan nodded and stood up to signal the end of the interview.

"I know you can handle this," he said, putting his arm around the younger man's shoulder and steering him toward the door. "And by the way," he added as Nick was leaving, "the next time you miss a press release like you did yesterday, you're fired."

"Terrible accident on my way to work . . ." Nick began.

Morgan laughed and pushed him out the door.

❖ **II** ❖

Words and numbers began to run around the cylinder at the center of the giant dome which was the Sifra-Messa spaceport. Nick read the printout with relief: the connecting shuttle from TGA flight 49803—the flight carrying the emissary from Alta-Ty—would be arriving on schedule. Thank goodness for that. He had been hanging around the spaceport all morning, drinking stimu-caffs, browsing at the magasette stand, inspecting spaceport mementos and souvenirs, and growing more and more nervous every minute. Silently he rehearsed the speech he had prepared as though it were a litany:

The Mutagen Corporation and the people of Sifra-Messa and of all the other planets in the Federation of Worlds extend to you their warmest welcomes . . .

Aliens were common on Sifra-Messa, but they kept to themselves and humans did little to encourage socializing. Incredibly, Nick had never before had dealings with one, aside from asking for the correct time, or for change of a credit bill. His inexperience made him all the more anxious. What if he slipped and made reference to one of those ugly, stupid clichés about aliens eating their children or popping out their eyeballs? He would have to be careful indeed.

Transgressions were particularly likely because the Alta-Tys had such an elaborate code of manners. According to a microfiche he had been reading ("Our Friends the Alta-Tyberians, Their Habits and Customs"), when a meeting took place between strangers a little ballet was performed before either party spoke a word. This included hand gestures, back bends, bows in which forehead scraped floor: they must have been extremely supple. When Nick tried imitating one of the illustrations in the microfiche, he nearly slipped a disc. He hoped the Alta-Ty would be understanding about the breach of manners.

. . . planets in the Federation of Worlds extend to you their warmest welcomes, and express every certainty that the genetic technology of the free galaxy will. . . .

One of the rituals, Nick noted with relief, was very similar

7

to a human custom: that of the host giving a present to the
visitor. The microfiche even described an appropriate gift, a
rala-senaya—a huge brush used to comb the cottony fur
which covered their bodies. The backs of the brushes tradi-
tionally featured colorful scenes from Alta-Ty folktales. Nick
had the modeling department at Mutagen build one and dec-
orate it with a human and an Alta-Ty united by a double helix—the Mutagen logo. He carried it now in a box under his
arm.

More information was appearing on the cylinder: passengers from flight 49803 had cleared DeContam and Customs
and were entering the central dome through Gate 12. Nick
ran a hand through his thick black hair and hurried to the
gate, where a crowd was already beginning to form.

. . . *certainty that the genetic technology of the free
galaxy will find a speedy solution to the terrible tragedy
which* . . .

The entrance iris was dilating; the passengers, space-weary
after six months on board a cramped ship, were filing
through the gate.

. . . *the terrible tragedy which has befallen your
people. . . . The Mutagen Corporation and the people of Sifra Messa and of all the other planets* . . .

They were mostly pilgrims who, after years of watching
their favorite Lifestylers on holovision, were now determined
to see them in person. They came in tour groups led by
smiling guides, and it was easy to tell whom they worshipped: followers of Squire Stolid wore hats shaped like obe-
lisks, followers of Lex Largesse, gloves like huge hands.
Followers of Lady Lovelorn dragged their feet and lowered
their eyes, except to frown at the followers of twin 'stylers
Gloss 'n' Glitter, who were giggling and grabbing at one another lasciviously.

Then there were men in business capes, lawyers and ac-
countants and the others who kept the administrative end of
Mutagen in order, representatives from other corporations
with Mutagen accounts, and Federation tax auditors. Most
were human, but Nick noticed a sprinkling of aliens: Rooliks,
the craftiest businessmen in the galaxy, armed, no doubt, with
wild investment schemes for Mutagen capital; a few tiny
Wheezops who might be in for a size adjustment; five creatures with faces like fried eggs; and a willowy female whose
skin glittered with blue scintillae.

No Alta-Tyberians.

Nick waited a half hour more with mounting dread. Then he hunted up the flight steward and asked if there had been no Alta-Tyberians on board.

"Only Ms. Hasannah." The steward pointed to the willowy blue female, who was standing near the entrance iris, wearing an expression which might, on a human, indicate extreme irritation.

His voice dropped to a whisper. "She can't be an Alta-Ty—they're all hairy, like bears."

"Just the males," the steward said, laughing.

"Oh my God," Nick said, remembering this fact.

He thanked the steward and, summoning all his courage, charm and tact, approached the Alta-Ty.

"The Mutagen Corporation and the people of Sifra-Messa and of all the other planets in the—"

"You are from Mutagen?" Her English was perfect, but her voice scraped like an overtightened fiddle string. "I have been waiting one half hour. I sent a tachygram with the time of my arrival. I assume you did not get it."

"No, I did. But—"

"Then why were you not here waiting? Tell me that, please? I have been six months in space, on ships, off ships, at least I should be granted some common courtesy here, where my people are prepared to spend so many millions of credits, don't you think?"

"I'm terribly sorry. I can't *tell* you how sorry I am." He couldn't think straight; his mind was numb with panic. For a lack of something else to do he handed her the package he was carrying.

"Please . . . accept this . . . ?"

She looked at him for a minute; then her face softened and she said in a surprisingly mellow voice, "Thank you."

When she reached for it Nick noticed the cryogenic briefcase clipped to her wrist. It must have contained, under extreme refrigeration, the sperm samples and ovum, the future of her planet. No wonder she was overwrought. To have that responsibility . . .

"You must understand the strain I have felt," she said, tearing away the paper. "I'm sorry if I have been a trifle . . . ."

"Look, it's perfectly all right. I understand completely."

She opened the box. For an instant she looked puzzled; then the fury came back tenfold.

"What is this?" she hissed. "A humorous frolic at my expense? Dear sir, in case you do not know, I am a female, not a male!"

"There was no way to tell . . ."

She thrust the package back into his hands, turned and marched to the baggage pickup.

✿ III ✿

The MagLev cab sped along a copper ribbon inlaid in a graceful concrete arch, one of many that spanned the city. Powerful electromagnets supercooled in a helium bath to −450° F. held the car inches above the roadway, allowing it to slip along frictionless at fabulous speeds. Forward momentum was supplied by a linear induction motor and supplemented, at the passenger's request, by the thrust of a hydrogen booster.

Nick sat in a cushioned bucket seat in back watching the rock-candy towers of Averyville grow suffused with the glow of the setting sun. He could see Mutagen Labs in the distance, the mushroom-shaped buildings sharply defined against a background of soft green meadow and parkland. It was all very beautiful, and if he hadn't felt so awful, he might have enjoyed it. He glanced across at his alien guest, Hali Hasannah, who was holding the precious case in her lap and staring straight ahead, her lips a straight line, her eyes fixed on the back of the cabby's head.

"I'm . . ." he began, and saw it was useless.

At the moment she was concerned only with delivering the freezer case safely to Mutagen. Having carried it so many light-years she dared not allow a mishap now. Nick understood. He knew that time passed more slowly on a spaceship traveling at near-relativistic speeds. During her three-month galactic crossing twenty or thirty years might have elapsed on her home planet. If something happened to the samples in the freezer case, new samples might be another thirty years in arriving. And by the time the antidotal virus had been constructed and shipped back, the two or three Alta-Tyberians who were still alive might joke about it philosophically.

Nick studied her more closely. Her skin was sea-blue, so fine as to be almost transparent. The scintillation of light across it seemed to be caused by some sparkling oil, possibly cosmetic or else an effusion of the flesh. Her neck was long, thin and graceful; her face, surrounded by a halo of fleecy white hair, was dominated by huge almond eyes. Nose and mouth combined in a pliant beak, giving her the profile of a hawk. She wore billowy white robes which left her shoulders bare, and for jewelry a single sunstone stuck to her forehead.

How long, Nick wondered, would one have to stare at that face before it could be appreciated within its own aesthetic? Could a human ever see her thus? Or would he always judge her by human standards?

Human standards.

Her hands had four long fingers apiece, fingers grasping the edge of the freezer case so tightly that the ligaments stood out like wires.

"Faster, please, sir," she called to the cabby.

"Lady," the cabby called back, "I've got the booster on full—any faster and we'll jump the ribbon."

Even as he spoke the cab swerved dangerously; then Nick felt it tear free of the track. Robbed of its magnetic cushion, it dropped suddenly, stomach-wrenchingly, onto its auxiliary wheels. But at that speed wheels were no use. With a hideous squeal of rubber they skidded and spun. A rush of adrenalin accelerated Nick's brain until everything looked like a slow-motion movie: the other drivers beeping their horns, skimming out of the way; the looks of fright on their faces; Hali's scream piercing his ears like some high-pitched siren . . .

And he thought, with incredible calm, Oh my God, it's actually happening, we're going to crash. If we hit the guard rail slowly the emergency magnets will hold us there—but if we're going too fast we'll smash through and topple off the arch, eighty meters to the ground. We'll all be killed. And there's so much I haven't done! Why did I waste all that time working for Grim. . . ?

He felt as though minutes had passed; actually, it was only three seconds before they hit the guard rail and stuck there with a bone-rattling *thunk!* Airbags inflated into giant pillows, pinning them to their seats and cushioning the impact.

The doors sprang open. Nick punched down the airbags and grabbing Hali by the arm, pulled her out of the cab. Her arm felt as thin and light as a breadstick, and he worried it would crack under his grip. They staggered onto the concrete just as some short circuit ignited the upholstery; fabric and foam burned with an evil odor and a thick black smoke spewed from the open doors.

Hali was unsteady on her feet. Her entire body trembled. Nick helped her away from the wreck, back to a safe place where the cabby was standing, watching the column of smoke with misery.

"I just made the last down payment," he said.

Nick was consoling. "At least we got out alive. In a minute that fire will reach the hydrogen tank. We'd have been flash-fried— What?"

Hali was mumbling something. She stood beside him, hypnotized by the sight of the burning car. She mumbled it again:

"My briefcase . . ."

Nick glanced at her wrist. The case was gone; the broken strap hung there like a piece of modern jewelry. The next instant he was running across the concrete and then he was disappearing into the thick black smoke which billowed from the cab's doorways.

"Come back!" the cabby screamed. "You crazy?" Perhaps a half minute later he screamed, "Get out of there! It's going to blow up!"

Hali wrapped her long fingers into fists and pressed them to her mouth.

Meanwhile a MagLev fire truck and an ambulance were arriving along the emergency rail. Traffic had been cleared for a radius of two-hundred feet and drivers left their cars and sat on the hoods, silent, hungry-eyed, waiting for the bouquet of blood and singed flesh to spice their daily fare, to make their pulses race and furnish talk for the dinner table.

"He better get out of there," the cabby said to nobody in particular.

And out Nick tumbled, weaving and retching, clutching the briefcase to his chest. He staggered drunkenly some forty feet before the heat finally reached the hydrogen; then came the savage roar and the fireball, and the shock wave that knocked him on his face. Even as he fell he sheltered the briefcase with his body.

❖ IV ❖

"You have a visitor," the nurse said. She was an older woman, plump and pink, with sculptured white hair and an infuriatingly efficient manner.

"Who?"

Nick's voice was muffled; he had to lie on his belly on the waterbed so that the raspberry jam which had once been his back could heal. It might have been a lot worse. He had suffered only minor lesions from his fall on the concrete. However, the heat of the fireball had seared through his clothes and his skin, leaving him with third-degree burns from the back of his neck clear down to his calves. The area had been covered with synthi-skin—an antibiotic spongy material, to soak up the pus, backed by a microporous film which kept out bacteria. An electroanesthetic filament had been slipped into his spine; he should have been numb but the placement had been slightly off and instead he itched unbearably. Needless to say, he could not scratch. To Nick it seemed that this must be what the ancient Terrans had called "Hell," and despite his rational mind he found himself wondering what he had done to deserve it. Silly. The universe was a random occurrence on the road to entropy. Why look for sense or justice? Yet he did and came back, as man had for centuries, empty-handed.

"An alien."

Nick couldn't see the nurse wrinkle her nose in distaste, but he could detect it in her voice. He thought it funny that after living with aliens for so long people could still be bigoted. Fear of that which is different: the principle which keeps the small mind small.

"A lady with blue skin?" he said.

"Yes."

"Tell her I don't want to see her."

Even as he felt pleasure in reversing the situation—in making Hali the supplicant—he realized the pettiness of it. He had been hurt and he wanted to hurt back. He felt worse hearing the satisfaction in the nurse's voice:

"I certainly will!"

13

Morgan came by later that day with a box of candies. Nick declined, explaining that he was on a special diet to promote healing (doctors were only beginning to understand the importance of diet to recuperation).

"Too bad," Morgan said. He took a seat by the bed and popped a candy in his mouth. "That was beautiful. *Heroic.* When you saved that briefcase you saved a whole damned planet. That's something to be proud of. I think you should get a special commendation. In fact I recommended a promotion and a raise."

Morgan waited for the thanks. When none came he went on: "I can understand why you're angry. I heard about the scene at the spaceport. But Nicky, this is a job—it's not personal—and sometimes to do your job well you've got to swallow your pride." He put another candy in his mouth and chewed noisily. "You can't just tell an interstellar emissary that you don't feel like seeing her. Ms. Hasannah's a very sensitive lady."

"She's a cunt," Nick muttered.

"Maybe, but sensitive—and she was deeply hurt. She's holed up in her hotel room and won't talk to anybody. If it was up to me I'd say fuck her, but the men upstairs are busting my balls. They think this has the makings of a galactic incident. As a favor to me, Nicky. . . ?"

When Hali returned the next day he agreed to see her. He heard the rap of her heels entering the room, but no more sounds were forthcoming. Soon he began to wonder if she had changed her mind and crept away.

"Hello?" he said. "Are you there?"

Still nothing.

Painfully he raised his head to see the room. Sunlight streamed in a window, drawing a diagonal stripe across her form. As she watched him, tears spilled soundlessly from the corners of her great almond eyes. She looked so vulnerable, his resentment was replaced by an urge to comfort.

"Did you get the samples to the coldroom?"

"Yes." It was a small, choked sound. She seemed to be suffering each of his burns, over and over again.

"Look, don't cry, I'm perfectly all—hey! What are you doing?"

The waterbed sloshed as she knelt upon it, and the waves tipped Nick back and forth. Because of the electroanesthesia he felt only the itch; but he knew from the ripping sound that she was peeling away the sheets of synthetic skin.

"Don't do that, you'll open the wounds!" He tried to push her away, but he was weak and stiff-jointed and the roll of the waterbed swallowed up his motions. "Nurse!" he called in desperation. "Nurse, help me!"

"Hush," Hali said. "It will only take a moment."

Dear God, Nick thought, she's going to kill me, it's some weird Alta-Tyberian ritual, killing people to take them out of their pain. And there he was, helpless as a babe. "Nurse!" he screamed. "Goddammit . . ."

"Get away!" the nurse screeched, bustling into the room. "Get away from him . . . nobody's allowed to touch those dressings except Dr. Ornstein . . . get away this instant . . ."

Flustered, she hesitated. She looked as though she wanted to grab Hali physically but was afraid of touching the sparkling blue skin. Instead she poked the intercom and called, shrill-voiced and shaky, for the doctor.

On her way to the door, Hali paused to glare at the nurse. "You are unspeakably rude," she said, "even for a human."

Seconds after she left, Dr. Ornstein came bounding in.

"What's the commotion?"

"I saw it all," the nurse babbled. "The alien was rubbing her fingers on his wounds, and she tore off the synthi-skin. I tried to stop her but she wouldn't pay any attention . . ."

"Please, Ms. Hoening, try to calm yourself."

He went over to the bed and began to examine Nick's burns. Nick heard him draw in his breath and murmur, "Incredible."

"What?" Nick said. "What happened?" Although he already had a suspicion.

Later that day when they removed the electroanesthesia filament from his spine, Nick felt no pain. He reached behind and found his skin smooth, scarless. Next morning, still baffled but satisfied after numerous batteries of tests, Dr. Ornstein released him with a perfect bill of health.

❖ V ❖

Nick sent a note to Hali's hotel inviting her to a tour of Mutagen Labs and a progress report on the Alta-Ty problem. The information, he reasoned, would be so important she'd have to accept. Then he would have an opportunity to try to apologize for the disgraceful scene in the hospital. It looked to him as though their relationship was fast becoming a jumble of misinterpreted signals and responses overreacted to. He prayed he could make peace now while there was still a possibility of communication.

He was delighted to receive a message of her consent. He arrived at her doorstep wearing his best dress cape and carrying a bouquet of exquisite black orchids. Before ringing he ran a mental double-check; he couldn't afford another slipup. Everything seemed proper—right day, right time, lovely flowers—but what if flowers were an insult on Alta-Ty? What if they were given only to the crippled, or only on the occasion of a disaster, or only as the consolation for some great failure?

Take the risk or stand on the doorstep all day. He combed his hair with his fingers and rang.

Hali opened the door. She was wearing a dress of crinkly orange fabric, with sleeves that reached almost to the floor and spread like butterfly wings when she turned. They both began to speak at once.

"I must apologize—" she said.

"Please forgive—" he said.

Then they both laughed. It was the first time Nick had heard her laugh, and he liked it.

"I brought you these."

"Oh thank you, how very beautiful . . ."

Nick relaxed. Flowers, apparently, were a universal compliment.

She admired the delicate scrolls of the orchids, the black velvet texture. She held them to her nose and inhaled deeply, then she took a bite off one and chewed, a thoughtful wrinkle

16

on her brow. Her teeth were thick and flat and moved from side to side with a grinding motion. Presently she beamed.

"Delicious! I shouldn't, you know, I'm getting so fat . . ."

"You don't look fat to me." In fact he doubted if she weighed more than thirty-five kilograms.

"You fib."

"No, honestly. And how often do you get to eat foreign foods?"

"True. I will banish my worries."

"Good," Nick said.

"Would you like some?" She held up the remaining flowers.

"No, please. Enjoy."

Blissfully she took another bite. Then she asked Nick to excuse her while she finished her makeup, and retired to the bedroom. Nick, for want of something better to do, flicked on the holovision and sprawled across a lounger. A face appeared, a youthful sixty-year-old with crinkly eyes and a toothsome smile. The face was deeply lined and every line spelled kindness and concern over pressing moral issues. He was the father for whom, in this age of practical parthenogenesis, every man yearned. He was Johnny Quog, the Peace Party candidate for Federation president. And this must be, Nick concluded with a yawn, yet another political advertisement; the election was only weeks away. He kept watching through sheer apathy.

There are those among us today who are ashamed to be called human. They say we have destroyed ancient alien civilizations by imposing our own culture and morality. To them I say, Hogwash! I'm proud to be a human! And I don't think there's a race in the galaxy that couldn't benefit from a taste of old-fashioned human ways. I say, if alien races are benefiting from our wealth and technology, then don't they owe us something in return? As president, I shall propose a program of galactic acculturation—

"Who is that?" Hali asked. She was standing behind Nick, ready to go.

"The next president of the Federation." He stood up and switched off the set.

"I think he is paranoid."

"Oh?" Nick smiled. It amused him to see this glorified messenger from an insignificant world criticizing a man who

would soon be the principal figure in galactic politics. "Why
do you think so?"

She ticked the reasons off on her fingers.

"The racial chauvinism, the desire to impose his own
values on all others. His—what do you call it?—his *folk-
siness;* it is conspiratorial. It implies a 'you and I against
them' situation. Yes, I believe he is a very dangerous man."

"Well, don't worry about it. Our government has been a
stable democracy since 1776, and I don't think Johnny Quog
is going to be the man to upset it."

"Complacency," Hali said softly, "is the first step in the
fall of democracy."

That took away Nick's smile: messenger or not, she was
right.

Sitting in the back of the GE cab, Nick had an overwhelming desire to ask her how she had healed his wounds—but it
seemed somehow boorish, like questioning the quality of a
gift. Instead he said, "How did you learn to speak English so
well?"

"My people send groups of children to be educated on different worlds, to gain perfect knowledge of other cultures and
languages. These children grow up to be emissaries. When I
was a little girl I was chosen as an emissary to the English-
speaking worlds of the Federation. It was a great honor," she
added with uncertainty.

"What would you have rather done?"

"Stayed home with my family. Played with other children
like myself. Instead I lived with a human family and went to
school with human children. Human children. They were told
to treat me like one of their own and I'm sure they tried . . .
but I was so different and young people are so cruel."

She shook her head sadly.

PART II
A Tour of Mutagen

❖ 1 ❖

"These are the coldrooms," Nick said, watching Hali's reflection in the triple layer of insulated glass. The window gave a view of a cavernous room honeycombed with stacks of trays. Robots shuttled between the stacks, adding trays to some and removing them from others.

"It's refrigerated with liquid nitrogen," he continued, "to a temperature of −450° Fahrenheit. The trays they're carrying contain sperm, ova, blood samples, tissue cultures, amniotic fluid—occasionally whole zygotes—flown in from all over the galaxy. Naturally there's a backlog. The samples can wait here safely until their turn comes in analysis."

"The samples I brought," Hali said. "They are waiting here?"

"No, you have special priority. They're already in analysis. We'll see them in a few minutes."

They passed other coldrooms, "libraries," Nick explained, containing DNA sequences from the last two hundred years. If at some future date alterations in the gene pool showed unsuspected—and undesired—side effects, they could always fall back on these earlier specimens.

Further safeguards existed in the form of supercooled zygotes stored in caves deep below the surface of the planet. If a war or a galactic catastrophe ever did annihilate life, sophisticated machines would grow man anew from these seeds and educate him to build the world over.

"To what end?" Hali interrupted.

Nick thought for a moment. He had never considered the question before. "I don't know," he finally admitted. "Why explore new planets? Why break the genetic code? Why do anything? Why not just stand around and . . ."

Then he recalled that that was precisely what the Alta-Tys did, stood around on one foot and gazed into space. He left the sentence unfinished.

✣ II ✣

A uniformed attendant stopped them in the entrance hall of the next building and fed their badges into a validater. Satisfied, he said, "Clean building, Mr. Harmon, sterile suits required."

The suits were a disposable tissue-thin plastic sprayed with metallic paint to shield the wearer during radiation showers. They weighed only a few ounces and were quite comfortable as long as the room wasn't too hot (the "clean" labs at Mutagen were kept at 50° F. for just this reason). The popularity of the tights, cape and codpiece fashion stemmed from the fact that Mutagen workers could slip in and out of the sterile suits without taking time to undress.

Hali's dress was another matter.

"I think you'll have to take that off," Nick said, feeling a strange—and highly unprofessional—tingle of anticipation.

With no sign of shyness she slipped out of the dress and handed it to the attendant, who hung it in a closet alongside Nick's cape.

Underneath she wore a sheer, skin-tight tube of elastic fabric which reached from shoulder to hip. Nick couldn't help noticing how long and smooth her legs were, and he was surprised by the roundness of her hips and the small swells of her breasts. Before he had seen, in his opinion, a sufficient amount, she had shimmied into a sterile suit and the attendant was helping her position the helmet over her halo of cottony white hair and seal the clamps around the collar.

"Air comes through this filter disc," Nick explained, tapping the coin-sized grating at the base of the helmet. "This way we won't accidentally carry away any bacteria or viruses, and our own bacteria won't contaminate the experimental work."

"Showers to your left," the attendant said.

The door had a stepped edge covered with a thick gasket. It closed automatically behind them, sealing them in a narrow chamber some ten feet in length. A second sealed door lay at the opposite end of the chamber, an airlock configuration.

"Do this," Nick said, and covered his helmet almost completely with his arms. When Hali had imitated the position he pushed a lever on the floor with his toe. An indicator light went on and a moment later it blinked off.

"Ultraviolet radiation. It kills off everything—except us." Nick laughed nervously. The radiation showers were supposed to be harmless, but he had never been quite convinced.

Nick led her to a small table with a basin of liquid and a sponge floating in it, and sponged off both their helmets with a few quick wipes.

"Plain old ammonia. You hold your arms over your head to block the radiation. But then you need to do this so none of those nasty bacteria sneak by."

At the press of a button a second door opened and they entered the building proper.

"Why such precautions?" Hali asked.

"Did you ever hear of the Cancer Plague of 1989?"

"What is cancer?"

"It's a disease where cells start reproducing wildly for no apparent reason. Because it was one of the major killers of the twentieth century, a lot of researchers were working very hard to understand it. A common technique for examining cancer was to implant a carcinogenic DNA in an *E. coli* bacterium. Unfortunately the *E. coli* strain is very happy living in human intestines. All the labs had systems for biological containment, but the technology was primitive and the protocol was sloppy; somehow, some of the bacteria escaped. Because of the implantation, cancer, which usually isn't contagious, became highly contagious. A plague spread across Terra killing millions and millions of people."

"What happened?" Hali asked, her eyes wide with concern.

"A few months later a research team headed by a man named Chang found a general cancer cure. But since that time everybody's been very careful about containment."

He added thoughtfully, "Science has given us so many opportunities to destroy ourselves. Yet we survive and occasionally we even do some good."

They ascended Post 31 to the Theta level disc and walked along the curving corridor. Nick stopped at one of many doors and slipped his badge into the slot.

"Yes?"—a voice from the speaker grill.

"It's Nick Harmon. I have the emissary from Alta-Ty with me."

The door opened—gasketed like the previous one—and again they passed through an ultraviolet shower, through a second door and into a laboratory of spotless white walls and gleaming counters. Sterile-suited men were hunched over holocube terminals, measuring angles and making notes; others built models of sticks and plates and colored balls; still others operated centrifuges and sequinators, computer consoles and electro-phoresis windows where nucleotides settled like layers of sedimentary stone.

They were greeted by Paul Capek, a brilliant, intense man of forty, of whom it was rumored that he slept a scarce three hours a night, relaxed almost never, and subsisted almost entirely on a diet of stimu-caff and quik-snax. Of his sixty-six inches of height, three inches were shoe heel. He spoke in rapid-fire bursts of words, rarely pausing for breath. After some preliminary questions about how Hali was enjoying her stay on Sifra Messa (very much) and whether she had seen the Lifestylers yet (she hadn't but hoped to soon), he began his VIP presentation.

"This laboratory, like most of the other labs in this section, is devoted to the identification and analysis of problematic DNA sequences—that is to say, genes with some hereditary weakness, or genes that have mutated into something . . . undesirable. The latter being the case with your people. Since genes are always mutating—due to the effects of random radiation, pollution and chance—we have a saying, 'A genetic engineer's work is never done!' Ha, ha, ha."

Nick smiled weakly.

"Now," Capek continued with a fresh burst of energy, "let me show you what progress we have made with the Alta-Ty problem."

He led them to a viewscreen and began flicking switches. The lights in the lab dimmed and the screen lit up with two rows of things that looked like elbow macaroni.

"That is the karyotype—the pattern of chromosomes—for a normal human being. Forty-six chromosomes in all, twenty-three donated by either sex."

Another slide flashed on the screen, and this time one row of the pairs had an extra member.

"Human mongoloidism, the closest analogue we have to the Alta-Ty problem, occurs when the zygote receives three chromosomes in the twenty-one position, giving it a total of forty-seven—one extra."

Another slide. Both rows of macaroni were nearly a third longer, and the one on the left was divided into two equal groups. "This is the Alta-Tyberian karyotype. Seventy-two chromosomes, thirty-six from the female and eighteen apiece from each male."

"What?" Nick said.

"Two different males. Each Alta-Ty female needs two different males to reproduce. One male supplies eighteen chromosomes, the other supplies eighteen, the female supplies thirty-six."

"Far out," Nick said. He turned to Hali. "Two men and a woman . . . How do you do it? I mean, what are the logistics?"

Hali blushed and smiled. "It is less a problem of logistics than of finding three people who will love each other equally, without jealousy or competition."

Nick thought about the people he knew; how many did he love enough to have children with? Then he understood why the population of Alta-Ty was so small.

"And here is the Mongoloid Alta-Ty karyotype," Capek was saying.

"I can't see any difference," Nick said.

"There isn't any, at least not on this level. The problem rests *within* the genes, in the DNA sequence itself. So much for the trisomy analogue."

"Does that mean you cannot help us?" Hali asked, her voice tightening again, sliding up an awful octave and scraping like fingernails on slate.

"No, no, no," Capek said. "It simply means that we have more work to do. The problem is within the gene. You see, each chromosome represents approximately three-thousand genes. And each gene is a thread of DNA involving some thousand little message units. The units in the middle of the thread determine what enzyme will be produced, the units at the beginning and the end, when and how much. Any one of these little message units might be the cause of the aberration."

He led them to another machine, a dark metal cylinder

which reached all the way to the ceiling, and sat down at the holocube console next to it.

"This," he said, "is a photon microscope, the most powerful magnifying device we have. It's been interfaced to give a three-dimensional image in the holocube."

He pressed buttons and again the lab grew dark. Within the holocube a cloud of stars appeared.

"Those are the atoms. With the help of the computer we can make the electron bonds visible."

He pressed more buttons and fine lines appeared connecting the dots into a fabulously intricate web, a spiral staircase shape Nick recognized immediately as the double helix of DNA.

"Two hundred years ago," Capek said, "scientists would have given their lives to see what we're seeing now. DNA— the blueprint of life. That spiral structure contains all the necessary information for building a living, thinking, sentient being; for determining the color of his eyes, the shape of his nose, his intelligence and longevity, even his happiness."

For a time they gazed at the holocube and nobody said a word. Then Capek said, "The next step will be discovering what sequence of message units is responsible for the different Alta-Ty characteristics and finally locating the specific message units responsible for the deformity. The replicon men will take it from there."

❖ III ❖

On their way out of the building they relinquished their sterile suits to the attendant, who bundled them into a sterilizer. Hali put on her dress and Nick his cape, and together they stepped outside into the sunlight and fresh air.

Next, Nick said, they would be visiting a replicon shop. One of the very best replicon men had been assigned to the Alta-Ty problem, a genetic engineer named Hiram Scolpes—the same Scolpes who was responsible for the Scolpes Cipher, which

had made the awesomely complex prospects of totally synthesized polynucleotide chains an only frighteningly complex
actuality; the same Scolpes who had midwifed two of the
greatest Lifestylers of all time, Sir Etherium and Lex Largesse.
"You hold him in high regard," Hali remarked as they
crossed a green on their way to Post 51, where Scolpes was
located. "It is the first time I have detected enthusiasm in
your voice."
"Is it?" Nick laughed. Then he nodded. "When I was a kid
I used to go over to his laboratory and bother him with all
kinds of stupid questions. None of the other grownups would
waste time talking to me, but he was always kind and patient.
I guess he was the only adult I ever really admired. I wanted
to be just like him when I grew up. I wanted to be the
greatest genetic engineer ever and midwife Lifestylers and
win the Nobel Prize." Nick laughed again. "I even got as far
as medical school. I lasted four whole months."
"Why did you leave?"
"The work was too hard. I couldn't cut it—so I quit."
"And you took a nice easy job in public relations so your
mind could take a nap?"
"This isn't such an easy job," Nick said. "You have to deal
with Alta-Tyberian women who scream at you if you're five
minutes late—"
"*One half hour,* Mr. Harmon. You were one half hour
late, and I did not scream at you, I merely raised my voice."
"Pardon me," Nick said, and the way he said it made Hali
giggle. She reached out and squeezed his hand—four long
thin fingers, flesh slippery as silk, a wholly new sensation.
Nick felt the hair on the back of his neck stand up.
Because Dr. Scolpes was presently involved with viral
design and not actual synthesis, the work was mostly mathe-
matical and suitable for his office. Naturally this was far
more comfortable than his lab, where sterile suits and constant ultraviolet showers were required by law.
A Cyber 9000 computer, a microfiche scanner, a black-
board, a desk, a chair, a cot; these were the bedrock office
furnishings. Covering them like a layer of compost were
thousands of notepapers, loose microfiches and envelopes on
subjects as diverse as *The Political History of the Late 20th
Century* and *Teaching Your Dog to Communicate in a Sym-
bolic Language,* old-fashioned books with crumbling yellow

pages and peeling spines, molecular models dusty with age, mugs crusted with stimu-caff, technical magasettes and—this was one of Scolpes' passions—ancient cassettes of classical music played by artists with names like Oistrakh and Horowitz and Casals. (Scolpes had been known to say that his life's work would be completed if he ever found a gene for "musicianship"—then he would retire and spend the rest of his life learning to play the cello. Fortunately for mankind he was almost tone-deaf and the existence of said gene remained highly speculative.)

Dr. Scolpes was perhaps seventy. His tights bulged across a formidable belly; he leaned backward slightly to offset the weight of it, and his walk was a waddle. His head was bald on top with bushes of hair at the temples. Like many plump men his face was smooth of wrinkles—almost like a baby's—but the warm gray eyes showed more than a lifetime's wisdom.

He seemed genuinely pleased to see Nick; they greeted each other as old friends, or perhaps more like a favorite uncle and nephew.

Then Scolpes took Hali's hand and made a small bow.

"Delighted to meet my first Alta-Tyberian—and such a lovely one at that. Now I will explain to you what I do here. You must pardon me if I sound pompous, but you see I *am* pompous. It's a hazard of being a leader in one's field, a triple Nobel Prize winner, my dear."

He cleared his throat and smiled impishly.

"Now I take it the boys over in Post 31 have shown you how they analyze the structure of the DNA. Once each of the little strands has been identified according to the proteins they produce—the proteins which will eventually shape a human being or an Alta-Tyberian, in all their marvelous, mind-staggering complexity—the information is passed along to me. With the help of my faithful little computer"—he patted the aging Cyber 9000 affectionately—"I design the replicons which will do the actual work."

"*Replicons?*" Hali interrupted. "I hear that word again and again but I do not know the meaning. Could you explain?"

"Forgive me, my dear. A replicon is a sequence of DNA which can penetrate the cell wall and enter into the nucleus, where the original DNA resides, and maintain itself there, peacefully coexisting and recombining with the original DNA, subtly reshaping the function and purpose of the cell. The perfect house guest, so to speak. New cells create new structures; mutations are cured, longevity is increased, a third eye is added—whatever effect we are interested in achieving, within certain limits, of course.

"The actual mechanics are a bit less elegant than the theory. Once the computor has created the replicons, we add them to blood cells and cultivate them in an incubator. A small percentage of the replicons will become integrated into the blood cells. These 'improved' cells are separated from the rest and form the basis of the serum you will take back to your home world. Another ingredient in the serum is Growth Factor, which will accelerate the replacement of old cells in the body. This is how we will produce a generation of normal, healthy Alta-Tyberian babies."

Hali smiled.

"It is also," Scolpes continued, "the essence of how we make a man into a Lifestyler. However, in the case of the Lifestylers we aspire to a norm of our own creation. Rather like playing God and trying to beat him at his own game. We attempt to arrange the message units within a strand of DNA in such a way that the resultant being will appear as we have imagined him in our daydreams—and in our nightmares. It is the most difficult sort of *prediction* one can imagine, nearly as haphazard as predicting the shape of a tree by a glance at the seed. We fail often," he added, a distant look in his eyes. Then he said to Hali, "Have you seen the Lifestylers yet?"

Hali shook her head. "I look forward to it."

"You must take her to see them, Nicholas."

"The trip's all planned. We leave Friday. Lex's temple is first stop."

"Ah—then you could do me a very great favor. I spoke to Lex this morning. He said he had something to discuss with me—it had to do with the coming elections—but he was afraid to talk on the phone. He wanted me to drop everything and run over to the temple. I told him I couldn't possibly because of the rush on the Alta-Ty job, but as soon as I'd finished I would be in touch. You must understand, my dear Ms. Hasannah, that the Lifestylers are half god, half superstar and used to being coddled. If I ran off every time Lex or Sir Etherium called, I'd never get any work done. Often the only thing bothering them is their own neurotic fantasies and by the time I see them they've forgotten all about it. Nicholas, you know Lex personally and he trusts you. You could go backstage after services, find out what's bothering him and personally relay the message to me—*if* it's something important. Would you mind?"

"I'd be honored," Nick said.

IV

After lunching at the Mutagen commissary—Hali hardly touched her food—Nick decided to shorten what remained of the tour as much as possible. Having little understanding of Alta-Ty psychology, he could not know if Hali was getting depressed about the destiny of her people, or if she was suffering what certain humans suffered while touring Mutagen: vague feelings of uneasiness over man's tampering with cellular stuff. Either way, she did not look well.

They strolled through a central garden, past fountains and a grazing unicorn. The afternoon was cooler; the buildings surrounding them cast squat mushroom shadows, and far away the towers of Averyville sparkled like rock sugar.

"There's not much else to see," Nick lied.

"I've seen so much already my head is spinning—oh!"

They had come across a bed of violets and daffodils.

"Do you think," Hali asked, "anyone would mind?"

"I don't think so."

She plucked a violet and bit off a petal. Immediately she looked happier. Nick made a mental note for next time.

"See that building over there?"

Hali nodded.

"That's where we do cloning."

"What is that?"

"A clone is made by removing the nucleus of a human cell—any cell, practically—and inserting it in an egg cell in which the nucleus has been destroyed. The egg cell grows into a perfect copy of the donor of the nucleus. In other words, you could take a scraping of my skin and grow a whole army of Nick Harmons from it. I don't know why you'd want to. They wouldn't be very good fighters."

"But they would be cute," Hali murmured.

Nick glanced at her; then he looked at his feet and colored slightly.

"Anyway, you get the idea. Cloning is prohibited by law, except in special circumstances—otherwise it would stagnate the gene pool. For example, thirty years ago a man named Harry Peretz was generally considered the greatest rocket polo player who ever lived. We cloned an entire team from him, seventeen men. In addition to being fabulous athletes, they seem to be able to read each other's minds, the way identical twins sometimes do (like identical twins, they're all grown from the same cell), and that's why we've won the Olympics for the last six years.

"And over there is the brain building. Despite breakthroughs in microminiaturization, cyberneticists never have been able to build a brain as cheap and efficient as an organic one. Instead we grow brains that can be interfaced with traditional computer hardware. Of course they're not like our brains—they're not conscious, not in the human sense. Among other projects, we're working on a guidance system for the new starships that will be entirely organic and self-repairing. Maybe someday we'll be able to grow a whole starship from scratch!

"Those low buildings to the left are storage for the donor doubles. For centuries doctors have had trouble doing transplants because of the body's tendency to reject foreign tissue. Since Mutagen began offering the service, parents-to-be have had the option of twinning the zygote—turning the fertilized ova into identical twins. One grows up as a normal human being, the other is put into storage to serve as a donor double. A source of spare parts, to put it crudely. Organs, limbs and tissue are, naturally, the correct size and shape, and since they grow from the same cell, the body won't reject them."

Hali was looking at him strangely. "Do you have a . . . donor double?"

"As a matter of fact I do. See these three fingers?" He raised his hand. "Crushed playing rocket polo. They're replacements from my donor double."

"Pardon my boldness," Hali said, "but the donor double—doesn't he mind?"

"He can't mind—he's kept asleep all his life."

"Are you certain?"

"Of course I'm certain," Nick said irritably. "They keep him drugged."

"Have you ever seen him?"

"No, you're not supposed to. It can be psychologically damaging."

"But in truth he is a man like yourself."

"No." Nick tried to be patient. "He was artificially created. If my parents hadn't had the zygote twinned, he wouldn't exist."

"Or else"—she smiled slightly—"you wouldn't. Am I mistaken in believing that identical twins are brothers and neither is the original?"

Nick had never thought of it that way; now he had a vision, a man like himself locked in a long black box, feeding and excreting through tubes and exercised by machines, half existing in a twilight dream while organs were plucked from his body like ripe fruit.

❖ V ❖

"One more thing to show you before we go back to the hotel."

They had left the laboratory compound, passed the security gate out into the surrounding gardens where the general public were permitted to visit. Crowds of tourists, human and alien, swarmed about the visitors' kiosks buying plastic icons of their favorite Lifestylers, little chains of DNA in transparent domes, holoslides of the Mutagen Labs. Nick pushed his way through, making a path for Hali, and they took a place on the slidewalk.

"Where are we going?"

"To the zoo. It's a brand-new exhibit—they just built it this year."

"Ah! There was a zoo on Terra I visited often, the San Diego zoo. The sight of bears and lions and elephants gave me great pleasure."

"This is a different kind of zoo."

"What kind?"

"You'll see."

The slidewalk carried them past a row of cages: an elephant only two feet tall and shocking pink in color; a mahogany cockroach the size of a car which skittered along the walls with quivering antenna; a dog with gills to breathe underwater; and a fish which walked, not very comfortably it seemed, on land.

Nick explained how these "hybrids" had been developed from existing animals by altering the DNA. They were fanciful creations, like the Lifestylers, devised with no purpose in mind but to charm and intrigue the observer.

Next the slidewalk brought them to a place where they could ride a "Pegasus"—a flying horse tethered on several hundred yards of line—for five credits. Nick goaded her, but Hali didn't have the nerve. It looked too precarious, way up in the air, supported by those two stubby wings.

The slidewalk dipped into a shallow valley. Deep ravines had been dug, leaving islands a quarter mile in diameter, landscaped with ferns like great lacy fans, and seething, bubbling swamps. Weather generators laid a blanket of mist across the floor of the valley and drove the temperature up to 90°.

"At the San Diego zoo," Hali said, "they had llamas. Have you ever seen a llama?"

Nick shook his head.

"They are horselike beasts, noble and distinguished yet terribly stupid, always reminding me of certain pompous humans. My people believe that the Maker made animals to help us laugh at ourselves. I could not help but laugh when I—*oh my goodness!*"

Hali grabbed onto Nick's cape and hid her head against his chest.

He laughed. "It's okay, it can't hurt you."

"But what in the name of heaven is it?"

She peeked from the shelter of his cape; seeing that the hideous creature was confined by a ravine, she loosened her hold on him. Now she let go altogether, pulled herself erect and tried to recover some of her dignity.

The beast which had appeared from behind one of the rock walls was easily twenty feet tall and nearly forty-five feet in length, counting the tail it leaned on for support. Its legs were massive pistons, its arms grotesquely delicate and its gaping mouth jammed with ivory daggers. Scaly skin hanging loose across its body shimmied as it scurried to the edge of the ravine.

"Yes, and what did you say this creature is?" Hali asked, struggling to maintain her composure.

"It's a Terran reptile called tyrannosaurus rex, which became extinct seventy million years ago!" Nick was bubbling over with enthusiasm. "Remember what I told you about clones?"

Hali nodded but couldn't seem to find her voice.

"Well, Terran archaeologists found a scrap of tyrannosaurus skin sealed in resin. They sent it to us and we took the nuclei from the cells and embedded them in alligator egg cells. One of them took and grew up to be Lambie Pie here—that's what we call her."

Perhaps the mention of the name triggered a response in that pea-size brain, for now Lambie Pie leaned across the ravine and took a swipe with one three-fingered claw. The talons were like sickles.

"How nice," Hali said. "Perhaps we should be going."

"The brontosaurus is about twice that size."

"We will see him next time," she said firmly and, seizing Nick by the cape sleeve, pulled him back to the slidewalk.

VI

That night Senator Harry Harmon was holding a reception in Hali's honor. She invited Nick to escort her and reluctantly he agreed. As they rode in a MagLev cab to the senator's mansion at the outskirts of Averyville, she asked if Nick were any relation to the important statesman.

"He's my father," Nick replied.

"I am glad to know it!"

"Why?"

"Because if he is your father, then he must be a man of qualities. I was worried that the reception would be only politicians, men who, as my people say, trade love for power."

She had changed into layers of long gauzy sheaths, each a different pastel shade, like the skirts of a rainbow jellyfish.

Her eyes were outlined in black and a golden sunstone gleamed from her forehead. The scintillation of her skin was such that she appeared to be illuminated from within.

"Love for power," Nick murmured. "That's a pretty good description of the senator."

Nick was wearing his best jeweled codpiece, knee-high dress boots and a flashy turquoise cape embroidered with symbols of the Lifestylers. The odor of his new musk après-depilatory cream was a little overwhelming.

"What about politicians on Alta-Ty?" Nick asked.

"There are no politicians on Alta-Ty."

"No? Who runs the government?"

"There is no government."

"Then how," Nick asked, upset, "do you get anything done?"

"I might better ask the question of you." Hali smiled.

"But what about group decisions? I mean, who decided that you would be an emissary?"

"Everyone."

"Yes, but how? Everyone on the planet didn't suddenly agree to send you. Did they?"

"Not precisely. The decision took several weeks. You must understand, Mr. Harmon, Alta-Tyberians are very different from humans. I may not seem so, but I was raised with humans.

"Humans argue, this I have observed. Whenever anyone has an idea someone else appears to propose the opposite. Everywhere there are dualities. You are divided into two empires, the Federation and the Alliance, and two parties within the Federation. Within the parties, I am given to understand, there is a liberal faction and a conservative one, and within the liberal a right and left wing. And so forth and so on. Endless dualities. It is because for you arguing is a way to fortify the ego. Discord makes you feel stronger; dissent gives you the illusion of being more alive.

"For us it is different. That which is for the good of the people is obvious. Most of the time we are all in agreement. When we are in doubt about some new venture, we think about it until the doubts are cleared away."

Now was the time, Nick decided, to ask the question which had been bothering him since the day in the hospital. It took a bit of courage.

"Do you"—he cleared his throat—"have psychic powers?"

And the unvoiced question: Had his innermost soul been open to her all this time? Had she glimpsed the frightened child who dwelt within the big, handsome, easygoing shell that people believed to be Nick Harmon?

Hali smiled. "No, no more than you humans." (Evasive remark, that.) "But you erect barriers. Each of you carries around his own little fortress and an armory of arguments to defend it. On Alta-Tyberia we . . ." She searched for the word. "Meld."

"And there's never one Alta-Ty who wants to control all the rest?"

"On rare, rare occasions."

"What happens then?"

"We try to heal him."

"We do have leaders," she said, a while later.

"Ah."

"But they are not political, not in the human sense. They do not wield power, except the power accorded to them by their age and experience. Mainly they advise."

"I see," Nick said. "Elders of the tribe, sort of?"

"Sort of."

"How old are they?"

"Oh, thousands and thousands of years."

"I don't understand."

"They return from beyond the chasm of death to help us in times of crises. Alas, they come only rarely, for it is a great suffering to be born into a body of flesh."

Weird, Nick thought, but said nothing.

Hali continued. "It was one of these advisers who told us to seek help after the comet came and our infants began to . . . change."

"You needed an adviser to tell you that?"

"Yes. We had intended to perish, but the adviser told us it was not yet time. He told us to seek your help."

"And you would have just perished otherwise?"

"We are a very old people," Hali said. "Everything has a time to die."

❖ VII ❖

"Good evening, Mr. Harmon," the doorman said, opening the cab for them.

"Hello, William," Nick said. "How's stuff?"

"Fine, and yourself?"

"No complaints."

"You haven't been to the mansion in a long time. Your father will be pleased to see you."

"That, William, I doubt."

Nick helped Hali from the cab and up the front steps. The senator's mansion was a rambling ivory castle of towers and arches which merged in soft curves and sculptured loops, as if pulled from toffee.

"How splendid!" Hali whispered as they entered the vestibule. Their feet sank into swirling carpetgrass from Altair, and overhead a fabulous chandelier of Cebeian rain crystals seemed suspended by magic. A winding staircase carried them to the second floor, and they strolled toward an enormous room at the end of the hall. From it issued gay voices, and a Bucla band playing rich sine-wave harmonies.

"Are you well?" Hali asked with concern. "You seem to be in pain."

"I dread going in there. I dread seeing my father and all his bullshit politico friends."

"You mustn't feel that way."

"You've never been to one of these receptions," Nick said.

"Oh yes, growing up on Terra I was often invited to political receptions."

"And you like them?" Nick asked in disbelief.

"It is my duty as emissary. The sweaty hands, the platitudinous conversation, the dreadful little meatballs—yes, I enjoy them immensely."

Nick laughed. "Those meatballs! You mean they have them on Terra too?"

"Mr. Harmon, I am sure that everywhere in the galaxy man goes he brings with him little meatballs."

"Anytime you feel like leaving," Nick said, "just give me a nod."

Reaching the ballroom, they hesitated at the entrance, like swimmers reluctant to plunge into icy waters. Men and women in opulent evening dress were gathered at the side of the room exchanging choice gossip; others crossed the center of the floor in sedate file, performing a dance which was the latest thing from Terra. All the best families were there, the pick of Averyville society. Nick saw many women he knew being wooed by troops of handsome gigolos, hired for the occasion, while their husbands and fathers talked business in the "smoke-filled room" across the hall. Such were the conventions of Averyville entertaining.

He took Hali's arm, and together they entered. Heads turned, conversations ceased in mid-anecdote. He heard somebody whisper, "Look . . ."

They were a striking couple all right, blue skin and white, white hair and black, both of them over six feet tall. But that wasn't it. Most of the guests didn't know that Hali was Nick's "assignment"; they thought the involvement was romantic, at least they *hoped* so, for a scandal of that proportion would fuel the fires of Averyville gossip for the next year.

Senator Harmon's son and an alien . . .

Nick saw a figure cutting through the crowd. "Oh no," he murmured.

"Nicky, where *have* you been?"—she was eighteen, a bubble of blond hair, a pert, turned-up nose and a rosebud mouth. Her eyes were baby-blue and calculating, her dress pink chiffon. "We've missed you at the club."

"Well, you know . . ." Nick waved his hands vaguely.

"And *who* is this? You *must* introduce me."

"Hali Hasannah, Althea Clinger."

"It's *so* nice to meet you," Althea said. "I'll bet you're one of those exotic species the probe turned up. Do you do outrageous things like eat your children?"

"Only when we are extremely hungry. And what species are you, my dear? Tyrannosaurus rex, I would say, judging from your claws."

Althea gasped. "Why, I really—I never—"

"Later," Nick said and pulled Hali away.

"That," he continued, when they were out of earshot, "is the daughter of the chief of police, one of the ten most important men on the planet."

"And she is also your lover, yes? I will go apologize." She turned brusquely and started back. Nick grabbed her by the wrist.

"Not necessary," he whispered. Everybody was watching.

"Oh? And why not? Perhaps you too think she is a tyrannosaurus?"

"Look, it's none of your damn business what I think about Althea,"—a grin broke through, he couldn't help it—"though there is something a speck reptilian about her. You know, one night there was a dance at the club and I took another girl instead of her. She got so angry she had this friend of hers, Dorce, charge me with rape and assault. I spent twenty-four hours in jail before she announced it was a joke. Another day or two and they would have brain-wiped me."

Nick shook his head at the memory. "Let's pay our respects to my dad," he said, "and get out of here."

The "smoke-filled room" across the hall was half the size of the ballroom and twice as crowded. True to its name, gray tendrils rose from half a hundred joints and cigars and made a ceiling of soft blue smog. *Datura inoxia* was, judging from the bitter odor, the drug of the evening. In one corner a life-size holoprojection was in progress, a drama involving a half-dressed woman astronaut and an "alien"—actually a human male painted, embarrassingly enough, blue, with a shaven pate and a penis so long it trailed the ground like an airhose.

A butler passed with joints on a silver tray. Nick stuck two in his mouth, lit them from a silver lighter and offered one to Hali. She shook her head.

"You're sure?" he said. "It'll make the evening a little more bearable." He filled his lungs with smoke and nearly coughed his head off.

Now that their eyes had adjusted to the darkness they could see the men crowding the tables, smoking and drinking, playing cards and discussing the coming election and how it would affect their financial holdings.

The two of them worked their way across the room, tripping through the dense undergrowth of feet, stopping now and then while Nick greeted friends of the family.

Now they approached an old man who was sitting inside a giant plastic bell jar, suspended in some milky liquid like the remains of an amputated organ. His skin was yellow and shrunken so the eyeballs lay half-exposed in their sockets, and the lips, shriveled like dried peppers, left his teeth bare. The effect was, ironically, one of a huge grin.

Closer inspection would reveal hundreds of thousands of fine wires entering at the forehead, connecting the eight lobes of the cerebrum to a stereoscopic camera, a sensitive listening device, an olfactory sensor and a speaker grill; more connecting the three lobes of the cerebellum to a motor that steered the cube along on built-in wheels, at speeds up to twenty miles an hour.

Such an inspection would also turn up the tiny tubes which entered through the chest, introducing a mechanically oxygenated fluorocarbon emulsion into the left ventricle in place of blood. The pulmonary circulation, serving no purpose, had been disconnected.

A miraculous machine—who could argue?—self-contained, nuclear-powered and self-propelled, a feat of engineering which would have turned the ancient Egyptians, those mummy makers par excellence, green with envy.

"What is it?" Hali whispered, swallowing her horror.

"My father."

"But the machine . . . ?"

"A life preserver. It keeps his brain going and his body from rotting."

"You mean he's dead?"

"Sure. Most of our politicians have been dead for years."

The twin lenses of the stereoptic camera located atop the bell jar swiveled to focus on Nick and a voice like the grinding of ill-matched gears sounded, expressionless, from the speaker grill beneath it.

"Hello, Nicholas, what a pleasure."

Within the jar neither teeth nor lips nor jaw so much as quivered. The ultimate ventriloquist act, voice and body wholly disconnected.

"Hello, Pop," Nick said. "How are you?"

"How well can I be tied to this machine? If not for my duty as a public servant I would have myself disconnected. And you, Nicholas, are you feeling well? Have you been fired from the job yet?"

"You know damn well I've still got the job—or why would I be here with Ms. Hasannah?"

"Don't talk to me that way, Nicholas. If not for my influence you wouldn't have any job at all."

"Damn it, that's not true, there are a million jobs I could—"

"Quiet!—you're attracting attention. Ms. Hasannah, accept my apology for my son's lack of manners. He has never learned the respect for age which is, I believe, practiced on your own planet. And now I would like to introduce you to a friend of all Alta-Tyberians."

The stereoptic camera aimed at a nearby chair where a man of sixty was watching with amusement. Nick recognized him immediately, the fatherly grin, the crinkly flesh around the eyes. . . .

"Ms. Hasannah, the next president of the United Federation of Planets, Johnny Quog."

He rose from the chair and took her hand, his very presence radiating solace.

"I cannot begin to tell you," he said, "what an honor it is to meet the distinguished emissary from Alta-Tyberia. The Peace Party extends every consideration to you and your people during this terrible genetic crisis."

"Thank you." Hali dipped her head.

"It's difficult," the senator said, "to talk with all this noise. Let's move to the solarium—it's a bit more secluded."

"Sure," Nick said.

"I'm sorry, Nicholas, but we will be discussing matters of galactic security, highly confidential."

Nick nodded. "Fine. I'll wait here."

And he watched, allowing no sign of the rage welling within as Johnny Quog took Hali by the arm and Senator Harmon rolled along after them, motors whirring softly.

It was only twenty minutes before Hali returned. Meanwhile Nick had gotten himself involved in a game of hepticard draw with the mayor of Averyville and the chief of police—Bob Clinger, Althea's father—and lost 211 credits. He made a point of playing a few minutes longer before turning in his cards; he had waited for her, now she would wait for him. Outside, the doorman hailed them a MagLev cab.

Nick would not speak to Hali during the ride, nor would

he look at her. Instead he gazed out the window at the con-
stellations of light which were Averyville at night.

"Mr. Harmon," Hali said, "the feud between you and your
father is no reason why we should not be friends."

"What feud?" Nick grumbled. "There's no feud."

"I accompanied them because it is my duty, not because I
prefer their company. Now let us talk again and be friends."

"We're friends," Nick growled.

Hali sighed. "Mr. Harmon, how you vex me! Would you
like to know what we spoke of? Would that restore your con-
fidence?"

"Matters of galactic security—"

"Damn galactic security! The senator offered us full worldhood in the Federation. He said that if we had worldhood we
could qualify as a genetic disaster area and receive a hundred
billion credits in aid. I don't know if you are aware of it, Mr.
Harmon, but the cost of solving the Alta-Ty problem—if
there is a solution—and administering the antidote is astro-
nomical. We have no industry, no exports of value; in terms
of interstellar trade, we are impoverished!"

"What about the pallinite?" Nick murmured.

"Yes, the pallinite." Her voice grew heavy and bitter.
"That is certainly the solution. We will give you pallinite so
you humans, with your great wisdom and prudence, may determine the fate of life in our galaxy."

Now it was Hali's turn to be silent, Nick's to make
amends.

"I'm sorry," he said. "I guess I'm just selfish. I get all
caught up in my own little quarrels and forget what's at
stake for the Alta-Tyberians."

She grinned at him. "Let us forgive each other and be
done with it."

"Great."

"But tell me something. Your father, was he always so? I
find it difficult to believe that you are related. You are so in-
nocent and he is so . . . *calculating.*"

Nick sighed and was silent for a while, thinking. Then:
"He was a different person when Mom was alive, one of the
nicest guys you could imagine. He wasn't a politician then, he
was a genochemist like Scolpes—well, not like Scolpes, but
pretty damn good. He did some of the research that led to
curing manic-depression in humans. When I was eleven Mom

went back to Terra to visit Grandma and Grandpa and her ship was destroyed. It warped improperly and turned into antimatter, a one-in-a-million thing. My father didn't want to live any more. A couple of weeks later he got contaminated by an alien virus he was trying to crack. His bones turned soft and his body began to shrivel. His brain was all right, so they bottled him. And that's when he changed. All the compassion went out of him. That was also when he got interested in power and politics."

"Yes," Hali said sympathetically. "The soul leaves at death just as tenants vacate a crumbling house. No amount of clever machinery will make it stay."

"The soul?" Dimly Nick recalled it as a concept of preclassical Terran superstitions. "What is the soul?"

"That which makes us what we are."

"DNA, you mean?"

"Fine beyond DNA," Hali said. "Fine beyond time and space and the meddling of human fingers."

❖ VIII ❖

That was the last Nick saw of Hali for almost a week. He was too busy wrapping up assignments, canceling social engagements and otherwise clearing the next three weeks so that he would be free to show her the Lifestyler Temples. He hoped that by the time they returned the antidotal virus would be synthesized, the Alta-Tyberian race would be saved; the woman would be free to return to her home world and Nick to his normal routine. Nick had always resented anything that intruded on his normal routine. He couldn't understand why the prospect of this trip excited him so.

PART III
In the Temple
of the Lifestylers

❖ 1 ❖

The temple of Lifestyler Lex Largesse was located 800 miles southwest of Averyville on the Great Plain of Crick, a vast stretch of parched, scarred soil. Patches of scrub brush covered it like a threadbare carpet, and a plant that was not quite cactus waved sticky ribbons in the air, hoping to snare some of the plentiful insect life for lunch.

To the north, cliffs loomed hundreds of feet in the air, sheer sandstone walls streaked in sulfurous yellows and ochers and reds as dark as dried blood. At the base of one of these cliffs a bone-white wall marked off a semi-circular amphitheater some two miles in diameter. A pyramid of the same material bisected the wall and a winding slidewalk led from the pyramid entrance to a landing strip where tour buses, giant silver dragonfly shapes, settled one after the next.

So it appeared from the observation bubble of *Mutagen 5* at an altitude of 8,000 feet. The saucer-shaped ship was held aloft by an MHD—magnetohydrodynamic—drive, a system where interaction between a magnetic field of a superconducting coil and an electric field generated across an arc and caused air turbulence, which was converted to propulsion. (The full potential of electricity, so long neglected in favor of combustible fuels, had only recently been realized. High above the planet, orbiting panels of silicon cells thousands of acres in area converted sunlight to electricity and beamed it to the surface via microwaves, creating vast supplies of almost free energy.)

Within the ship's vari-tint bubble, which had been darkened to cut the glare of the desert sun, Nick sat at a control console easing forward the lever that reduced the j × B force and watching the altimeter register the descent. The ship was equipped with a sophisticated autopilot, but this was the first time Nick had ridden *Mutagen 5*—it was usually reserved for executive use—and he couldn't resist the opportunity to test his piloting skills.

Hali sat barefoot on the upholstered bench which circled

47

the cockpit, her knees pulled up to her chin, gazing at the curious structure below, the bone-white stadium and pyramid growing larger by the second, not with eagerness but with the anxiety of someone with uncompleted business. Try as she might to enjoy the tour, her heart was back in Averyville with the precious samples of Alta.

Nick was too busy to notice. He banked the saucer gently to the left, then leveled it again. Inside a bottle-shaped instrument a tiny simulacrum of the saucer approached the intersection of three cross-hairs. Then a blue light went on, signaling that he had locked into the landing vectors. The tension flowed out of him. Minutes later an almost imperceptible bump signaled touchdown.

A section of the saucer's underbelly folded down into a ramp and Nick and Hali emerged. They wore dark visors which barely cut the glare of the sun off the cliffs, and the hot dry air seemed to curl the insides of their nostrils. Immediately before them stretched an expanse of blacktop parked with rows of MagLev wagons and coupes, rocket tour buses and MHD campers.

Of the thousands of people milling about, the attention of at least a hundred was attracted by the couple's appearance. Tour groups wearing the large gloves which symbolized "Big-handed Lex" stared as though the two were the featured attraction; little children gaped while ice cream trickled down their shirt fronts, Rooliks aimed cameras and fired, *click, click, click, click, click.*

A human and an alien . . .

Nick wanted to duck back in the saucer; he wanted to shout, "It's not what you think, she's just my assignment!" He was, he saw then, just as bad as the rest of them, the nurse at the hospital, the shrewish society ladies with gossip like vinegar on their lips. He talked well and looked good in private, but faced with a crowd of strangers his foremost desire was to align himself with those who were alike and distance himself from she who was different.

He felt it but he was determined not to show it. He stuck out his chin and took Hali's arm, and together they marched regally down the landing ramp, across the blacktop and onto the slidewalk. In the distance the great white pyramid grew until they could read the sign over the isoceles door.

Entrance to the Temple of Lex Largesse
Welcome One and All
Altar, Gift Shop, Lifestyler Museum

On their way inside Nick dropped a twenty-credit bill into
the altar. He bought Hali a frostikoke and, at the gift stand,
a tiny platinum hand holding an even tinier house, a charm
to be worn from the neck on a chain. The schedule showed
that Lex wouldn't appear for another half hour; Nick suggested that they tour the Lifestyler museum in the meantime.

They followed a line of tourists down a darkened corridor
where fine laser-illuminated holograms (as opposed to the inferior "white light" variety used commercially) showed statues of classical Terra. These statues were called "sculptures,"
explained the tour guide, a pretty, buck-toothed brunette, and
were carved by "sculptors." Sculpture, she said, was an inferior art form which predated the invention of the Lifestylers. Since the sculptor worked in cold, static materials like
stone and steel, his sculpture could never grow or change; it
was temporally fixed, spatially frozen, lifeless. And the sculptor had to live with the awful frustration of knowing that he
could never transcend the subject-object relationship, that he
could never achieve true oneness with his work.

Inferior or not, Hali was deeply moved by a mother and
child composition, *The Pietà*, by Michelangelo, and Nick enjoyed the frank sensuality of Rodin's *The Kiss*. He was sad-
dened by Brancusi's *Bird in Flight*, since it obviously depicted
an extinct species, and astounded by a Giacometti nude
which bore an uncanny resemblance to Hali. Could this ancient Terran sculptor have been visited by Alta-Tyberians? It
seemed, somehow, unlikely.

The next exhibit featured the bust of a bald little man with
glasses and a cigar clamped between his teeth. Nick recognized him from the history 'fiches: Marvin Goldstein, "the
Father of the Lifestylers."

"Marvin lived in a Terran city called Los Angeles," the
guide said, beginning a prepared speech she knew as well as
she knew her own name, "and made movies dealing mainly
with copulation. He was called a *producer*—one who pro-
duces. In the spring of 1997 Marvin happened to see a newspaper article about modifying human beings . . ."

1997 was the year of the first star probe, the first time man dared cross the oceans of interstellar space. The early starships had tiny payload capacities, and genetic engineers had been put to work developing a diminutive man with minimal arms and no legs at all—he could weigh no more than thirty-five pounds—to pilot the crafts. Genetic engineering hadn't been in the papers much, not since the terrible Cancer Plague of 1989 halved the population of the country. The article Marvin read that morning was, in fact, the first public mention of human alteration.

Marvin reread the article, again and again. The technical details he did not understand, but the implications were clear to him; they made him tremble with excitement. Why not alter a man physically to enhance his talents? Immediately he placed a call to one of the scientists mentioned in the article and made his proposal.

No revolutionary idea was ever easily accepted. The scientist called him a "twisted degenerate" and hung up. But Marvin was not easily deterred. After all, the Neo-Decency League had been trying to stop display of his films for years, and he had never given in to them. For the next eight years the idea fermented in his brain. Then, quite by accident, he met Alexander Lebachuck.

Lebachuck had just been dismissed from Rockefeller University for altering humans without permission of the government's Genetic Review Board. Marvin offered to build a laboratory according to Lebachuck's specifications, sparing no expense on equipment (Marvin's films continued to be incredibly lucrative), and to pay him twice the salary he had been receiving—on the condition that he realize Marvin's concept.

They built their laboratory in a sparsely populated area of Los Angeles called Topanga Canyon. Naturally their initial work was primitive and crude. Their decision to make one simple bodily alteration for the first attempt might have stemmed, subconsciously at least, from one of Marvin's own problems. The result was Sam Super Stud. Marvin put him in a film called *Sam the Rammer* which was attacked, condemned and banned in every country on Terra. Needless to say, it did terrific business.

Marvin and Lebachuck barely had time to create their second Lifestyler, Rita Zowie, before the Los Angeles county sheriff's office broke into the lab, seized the equipment and put Marvin and Lebachuck under arrest for violating county ordinance 3982—practicing strange and unnatural alterations of the human form without sanction of the Genetic Review Board.

W. R. Silverman, one of the best civil-rights lawyers in the country, got them off with three years' suspended sentence, a million-dollar fine and a solemn promise never to repeat their crime on Terra.

Ten years had already elapsed since the first manned star probe had passed the orbit of Pluto. Warp routes had been discovered bringing thousands of G and K type stars within reach. Of these many had planetary systems, some had planets adaptable to human life, and eight had worlds where man could live in comfort.

Marvin took the most radical step of his radical career. Along with Sam Super Stud, Rita Zowie, Lebachuck and his nine assistants and four hundred crates of hideously expensive laboratory gear, he traveled to Sifra Messa, one of the pleasantest of the inhabitable worlds, and began his entertainment concerns anew beyond the jurisdiction of grandmotherly Terran rule.

Now, with an ever-expanding stable of Lifestylers, they began to crank out films in astounding number. The colonies gobbled them up. Even on Terra where the films were still illegal, millions of copies got by Customs.

In 2025 when the interstellar holovision relays were put in orbit, Marvin constructed a separate holovision studio for each of his Lifestylers, forerunners of the modern Lifestyler Temples. Broadcasts were jammed by Terra but the rest of the colonies watched avidly. Tourists began to make the long intersteller crossings just to see their favorite Lifestyler in person.

Meanwhile profits poured into Mutagen—for that was the name Lebachuck had chosen for the colony. Attracted by the glamour, the high salaries and the absence of Terran research restrictions, some of the best genetic engineers joined Lebachuck. Aspiring artists came from all over the galaxy with descriptions of "Concept Bodies," hoping that theirs would be judged an idea of merit and originality, of wit and charm, and that they themselves would be midwifed into their own creations. With such a concentration of talent, it was only a matter of time before Lifestyling became a true art form, in fact the greatest art form ever conceived of by man. Even conservative Terra finally acquiesced and allowed broadcasts to reach her hungry audiences. (Still, Lifestyling was not without its risks. "Creative synthesis" was one of the most difficult branches of genetic engineering; eighty percent of the potential Lifestylers died during rebirth or else lived out the rest of their lives improperly mutated, monsters and freaks.)

And so Marvin Goldstein lived to see his life's work legtimized. He died in 2039 of a heart attack, a result of overwork, and left his considerable fortune for genetic research in the service of humanity. At his funeral the president of the Federation of Worlds said:

"Every age has its prophet . . . who lights the heavens like a comet and passes on. . . . Marvin Goldstein was such a man. I look forward to seeing what improvements he will make on angel physiognomy."

"Lex will be appearing in a few minutes now," the tour guide said, consulting her watch. "The door on the left leads to the amphitheater. Take any seat you like. Have a wonderful time and thank you all for coming."

II

Nick and Hali moved through the rear exit of the pyramid and found themselves in the amphitheater they had seen from the air. It descended in front of them in steps, wide enough to serve as seats, and curved around on either side until the ends met the rock face. Indeed the majestic sandstone wall seemed to be the featured exhibit around which the amphitheater had been built.

Several hundred people were seated along the steps, some eating picnic lunches or scanning magasettes, others simply basking in the sun. Nick bought pillows from one of the many vendors who moved between the steps hawking their wares in various alien tongues, and ice cream, that classic Terran treat, from another. Then they found seats and waited, trying to lick the ice cream away before it melted.

Nick was squinting at the rock face intently.

"The arena is so big," she said, "will we be able to see him? Perhaps we should move closer?"

"Lex is big too," Nick said, without letting his eyes wander from the wall. "Alter the pituitary and man keeps growing and growing and growing."

"Do you mean to say he is . . . ?"

Nick held up a hand for silence. He whispered: "Look!"

At first she saw nothing. Then she thought she saw faint ripples emanating from a point seventy feet up the rock face, as waves spread from a pebble dropped in a pond, although it might have been her imagination or perhaps heat crazing the air.

A point appeared at the center of the waves, swelled to the size of a saucer and continued to grow. At first it looked like an opening in the wall, for our senses always try to explain phenomena in terms of the familiar. But as the hole grew bigger the truth could no longer be ignored: the hole was suspended in space some ten feet in front of the wall.

It cast a shadow.

Within the hole a palpable grayness could be seen, a fog to end all fogs. Yet unlike fog it did not drift from the mouth of the hole; the hole contained it. And ever larger it grew, now ten feet across, now twelve.

"What is it?" Hali whispered.

When Nick didn't answer she shook his arm in demand.

"Transdimensional window," he muttered.

"What's that?"

"Later . . ."

Hali gave up and turned her attention back to the hole. It had stabilized at a fifteen-foot diameter, although the edges continued to tremble and shift, defying her eyes to focus upon them. Within the hole, within the grayness, a form appeared, a dark, distant shadow. As it approached the mouth of the hole it gradually took on color and definition, first a figure vaguely human, then a face, finally an eye, an eye so huge that the pupil might have been a pond of ink and the blood vessels roots of trees reaching across the whites for nourishment. The eyelashes were thick as cables, the side of the nose, just visible along the left border of the hole, mountainous. The eye peered all around, like a little boy peeking through the knothole in a fence, trying to take in everything, then slipped upward to be replaced by an earthquake fissure of a mouth.

"Hello, pilgrims!" boomed a jolly voice.

"Hello, Lex!" they chorused in response.

"Glad to see you!" And you could tell by his voice that he really was. "I sure hope you've been giving to all your brothers and sisters—and your alien brothers and sisters too! By all means, give of your possessions. But don't forget the other kinds of giving. Try to *give of yourself*—that's the most important gift you have. Give your time, give your warmth, give your understanding. If we all reach out to one another the galaxy will be a little less lonely. It sure is a long way between the stars! I'll bet some of you pilgrims traveled a hundred light-years to be with me today."

The eye returned to survey the bleachers, then gave way for the mouth.

"Yup, I think I see some of my friends from Alpha Centauri."

A group of pilgrims cheered.

"And another group from Draconis—that must have been a long trip!"

"Sure was, Lex," one of them shouted, "but it was worth it!"

Lex chuckled and the ground shook.

"Hope you Rooliks brought enough film."

Everybody laughed. Roolik cameras had been clicking nonstop since the hole opened.

"Now, which one of my pilgrims would like a gift?"

The audience rose shouting "Me! me! me!" Some stood on their toes, others jumped for more height and raised their arms overhead. One jumping pilgrim slipped off the step and banged his head, but nobody seemed to notice.

"Now, now, no point in rioting. *Everybody* gets the gift of my love, and that's the most important thing I have."

The crowd quieted down and took seats. Lex's eye was circling the hole.

"The pilgrim on the bottom step, in the pink dress. That's right. Is your name Jianni?"

A girl with thick braids—she couldn't have been more than twelve—got shakily to her feet. She lowered her head in shyness and covered her face with her hands. The middle-aged man and woman sitting next to her, undoubtedly her

parents, whispered words of encouragement. Presently she
said, "Lex?" in a high, thin voice.
"I can hardly hear you," Lex said. "Tell me what you
want, and use a great big voice like mine."
"I'd like . . ." she began. "I'd like to go through the win-
dow and live in the other dimension with you."
Both parents stared at their daughter in surprise, and the
lines around Lex's mouth showed that he was puzzled too.
"What a strange request. Why would you want that,
Jianni?"
"Because—well, isn't it true that if you live on the other
side of the window you never grow old? I don't want to grow
old and have to die."
"You wouldn't like it on the other side," Lex said softly.
"It's cold and lonely here and you'd miss your parents. Anyway you've got to grow up and have children of your own.
When your death comes for you—and it won't be for many,
many years—you'll greet it like an old friend. Isn't there
something else you'd like, Jianni?"
Lex's mouth moved away from the hole, and out of the
grayness came a high-pitched whinny. A hand appeared, a
hand so enormous it could barely squeeze through the
transdimensional window. On the pink, fleshy pillows of the
palm stood a sleek chestnut Pegasus, the immature colt wings
drooping on either side.
Lex slipped his entire arm through the hole in order to
bring the back of his hand to the earth. The little girl ran forward and the Pegasus skipped off Lex's palm and trotted over
to meet her. She put her arms around its neck, pressing her
cheek against the soft fur, murmuring words of endearment.
Her parents joined her. Her father whispered something to
her and Jianni faced the window high above her head and
called, "Thank you, Lex! Thank you!"
"Take good care of him," Lex boomed.
While two priests led the party off the field, Lex singled
out his second Supplicant, a slump-shouldered, middle-aged
man whose one wish had always been for an expensive,
robo-chauffeured MagLev limo.
Lex's hand lowered a long, low-slung Victory Mark II, the
most expensive around. Sliding into the back seat, the pilgrim
was transformed; his shoulders squared, his head rose erect,
his face took on the expression of a world-weary playboy. To

see him being driven out of the amphitheater, one might have mistaken him for Federation Prez.

A young woman honeymooning with her husband request- ed, and received, a kitchen unit complete with dial-a-meal for her new home; a very old man was supplied with a robo- nurse so he would be less of a burden to his grown children. And so it went for the next hour, pilgrim after pilgrim mak- ing his request, large-handed Lex giving and giving and never exacting a favor in return, or a debt of gratitude.

"One last gift," Lex said. "Who will it be?"

"Me! Me! Me!" everybody was shouting.

He chose a teenage boy who wanted a starship. It was al- ways the children who asked for impossible things; requests the adults made were always fulfillable, boringly so.

"Wouldn't fit through the window," Lex apologized. "Any- way, a starship's a big responsibility—you're planning to join the spaceforce, aren't you?"

The boy looked startled. "How'd you know?"

"I've got my ways. Seven or eight years from now, *if* you keep up your studies, the Federation may make you pilot of your own starship. Think you can wait that long?"

"Yeah." Without much enthusiasm.

"In the meantime you can practice on one of these."

Lex's hand came out of the hole holding a championship- model skimmer, every teenage boy's dream. Gingerly the giant hand passed it to the two little hands, and any disap- pointment was lost in the sparkle of sun on polished steel.

Lex withdrew his arm through the window—then stopped at the wrist.

Over the course of a lifetime the performer perfects his act. Problem spots are edited, routines ironed out. An economy prevails where every gesture has a purpose and ev- ery superfluous gesture has been eliminated. Unnecessary mo- tions, no matter how slight, are noticed by the sensitive viewer.

Nick, raised on the Lifestylers, knew there was something wrong. He couldn't define it, he simply *knew*. Lex shouldn't have hesitated at the wrist, he should have drawn in his hand. What was going on?

The hand seemed to be stuck outside the hole. It turned and twisted, it narrowed itself and made a fist; still it could not withdraw. Nick thought he saw a bracelet of green light holding it in place like a handcuff, but the sun was so brilliant he could not be sure. Soon the hand was struggling like a trapped animal, and the audience, receiving the message of panic, became all abuzz with low anxious voices and nervous laughter.

"Something's wrong," somebody cried, and somebody else, "Get help!"

Several priests appeared at the door of the bottom of the bleachers, watched for a moment, then hurried back inside.

Nick felt Hali's hand tighten around his arm.

"What is it?" she whispered.

"I don't know, it's never happened before. He seems to be—"

Nick didn't finish, for at that moment a blade of green light flashed beneath Lex's wrist and his skin curled back along a deep gash. Jets of arterial blood, brilliantly red, squirted seventy feet to the ground and sizzled against the parched earth. The puddle grew to a pond, fed by the nightmare waterfall, and the pond crept leisurely toward the bleachers, edges curled with surface tension like some vast scarlet amoeba eating up the desert.

Everyone was screaming and running every which way. Nick alone seemed to have kept his head. He tried to get Hali's attention, but she had retreated into a kind of shock; her eyes were locked on the bleeding wrist, her body was rigid and shaking. Nick slapped her lightly across the face to no effect. He lifted her in his arms—she couldn't have weighed more than thirty-five kilograms—and carried her along the steps, avoiding the pilgrims, who were running every which way without sense or purpose. One man pushed a woman aside and she tumbled down the steps, over the rail, into the sea of blood, which had by now spread to the foot of the bleachers. When she rose to her feet she was covered with blood from head to toe and her eyes and her mouth were three gaping black holes.

High above her the hand of Lex Largesse twitched spasmodically and then hung limp from its transdimensional window.

❖ III ❖

Mutagen 5 had three decks, the lowermost divided like a pie into three staterooms. Nick carried Hali into the room she had been using and laid her gently on the bed. Gradually her shaking subsided. He brought a jigger of brandy from the galley and, sitting on the bedside and supporting her head with one hand, trickled it between her lips.

It worked; she gagged and shuddered and then she was convulsed with a terrible fit of coughing.

"Easy," Nick said. "Easy."

She looked so fragile he was afraid she would cough herself to pieces. He put an arm around her shoulder and held her while she sipped some more.

"The blood . . ." she whispered.

"Don't think about it."

"It was not an illusion, was it? Not part of the performance?"

Nick shook his head.

"Then he is dead?"

Nick nodded. "I think so. Is there anything I can get you?"

"Sleep—let me sleep."

He covered her with a blanket and watched as her breath slowed and finally became rhythmic, the healing breath of sleep. Then he waited a little longer. What he had to do next he didn't look forward to at all.

Upstairs on the second deck he plugged a holocube into the phone interface—eye contact might make it easier—and punched Scolpes' personal code at Mutagen. Nick identified himself to the robo-sec and in a moment the bald smooth face filled the screen, the wise gray eyes smiled at him. In the background Nick could hear the frenzied violins of a classical Terran orchestra and a woman howling in some foreign tongue. He felt miserable at having interrupted Scolpes during one of his rare moments of relaxation.

"Hey, Doc, I'm sorry to disturb you . . ."

"Don't be silly, Nicholas, it's always a pleasure. What do you think? Von Karajan conducting Wagner's *Die*

58

Götterdämmerung. Exquisite, yes? The fall of the gods, the destruction of Valhalla. Listen to that woman's voice!"

It sounded to Nick as though she were in terrible pain. He had never been able to understand the aesthetic of Terran music with all its emotional excess, its thunderings and weepings and moanings. But he nodded anyway.

"Just great, but could you turn it down a little? I've got something very important . . ."

"Of course! One minute."

Scolpes' head vanished and the music ceased abruptly. His head reentered the cube and Nick continued against the even more difficult background of silence.

"I'm here at Lex's temple—"

"You went backstage after services and he told you he'd forgotten entirely why he called me—am I correct? They are such children! I hope you passed on my regards?"

"Please, let me finish. I didn't pass on your regards because, you see . . ." Nick hesitated, first phrasing it carefully in his mind. "I didn't get a chance to talk to him. During services he was . . . he was killed. I don't know if it was an accident or what."

"Killed? No."

"Yes, I saw it with my own eyes. There's no possibility of mistake. I'm sorry."

"My God. Excuse me, Nicholas."

The head turned gray and faded from the cube; however, a yellow light showed that the circuit had not been disconnected.

"Are you still there?" Nick asked.

"Yes, yes." The voice was one of anguish; he was a father who had lost a favorite son, an artist who had seen a work in which he had participated slashed to ribbons; and the emotions of his face must have been such that he did not wish to display them on the cold circuitry of a holocube.

"How did it happen?" he said, after a long silence.

Nick described all he had seen. At a certain point Scolpes stopped him.

"A bracelet of green light around his wrist?"

"As far as I could tell. It all happened very fast. Does that suggest anything to you?"

"As far as I know a phenomenon of that description could only be produced by a psychic field amplifier."

"I thought the psych field amp was just a theoretical concept," Nick said.

"Gracious, no. I was invited to consult on the prototype. It was successfully constructed but nobody had sufficient concentration to operate it."

"Then you think it could be murder?"

"Most assuredly." Scolpes' voice had regained some of its composure. "And I suspect that Lex was murdered to prevent him from telling me whatever it was he had planned to tell me. If only I had taken his request more seriously."

"Didn't you say nobody had the concentration?"

"Nobody we could find. But the galaxy is a big place with many sentient inhabitants. Do me a favor, Nicholas. Go to Sir Etherium's temple as soon as you can. See if he knows what was troubling Lex. After all, they were very close friends."

Nick asked how the antidotal virus was progressing, hoping for some good news to tell Hali, but all Scolpes would say was that work was coming slowly.

Nick promised to leave for Sir Etherium's temple that night and made other efforts to console Scolpes. He had never been very good at consoling others for their losses, since he himself was so terrified by the thought of the life machinery grinding to a stop, the cessation of consciousness, the endless black nothingness he believed to be death. Occasionally the realization that he was not excluded, that he was mortal, that it would someday happen to him—the realization of this made his head reel.

❖ IV ❖

Nick was sitting in the galley on the second deck drinking stimu-caff and plotting a course to Sir Etherium's temple when Hali came up the stairway. Her bare feet were silent, her blue skin almost invisible in the shadows; but the huge almond eyes, gathering ambient light, shone like suns. She cleared her throat and he jumped, spilling stimu-caff all over the maps.

"I am sorry if I—"

"Forget it," he said, mopping up the liquid. "How are you feeling?"

"Better. I would like some fresh air."

"Good idea. Let's take a walk."

It was chilly as they set off across the landing strip. Although the sun had set, several MagLev wagons and campers were still parked while families ate picnic suppers and savored the evening air. Soon they were walking along the rough sandstone, the lights from the pyramid fading behind them. Overhead the Milky Way was fabulous. Schleiden, the larger of the two moons, sat on the horizon glowing a mystical yellow while small red Schwann raced madly across the heavens as it did four times a night.

Nick told her about his call to Scolpes and asked if she would mind continuing the tour as planned; otherwise he could ferry her back to Averyville and continue by himself.

"No, no, it is not necessary," she said. "I feel better now. The night is beautiful and the air clears my head."

After a while she continued, "It was simply the sight of him trapped there and wounded and helpless, with nothing to do but wait while the blood ran out of him. . . . It reminded me of my own people, trapped . . ."

She began to shake again. Nick put his arm around her and she melted into his breast. She raised her face, a blue oval of a moon, her eyelids fluttering, closing. The lips of her "beak" were hard and smooth—yet pliant—when he kissed her. She opened them slightly and the inside of her mouth had a salty taste. His tongue entered hesitantly, ignorant of the rules. Her teeth felt broad and flat; they parted slightly and the rough tip of her tongue, uncoiling like a snake, touched his.

He felt a tremor pass through her. He tried to kiss her again but she pulled away, shaking her head. "Come," she said, and taking his arm, began back toward the cruiser.

"Did I do something wrong?" Nick said.

"No."

They walked and walked and Nick felt a desperate desire to say something, anything. Finally, stupidly:

"Have you ever kissed a human before?"

"No, certainly not. For the ten years I lived on Terra I practiced on oranges."

"I forgot about—"

"As a matter of fact, Mr. Harmon, I have kissed innumerable humans." Her voice was getting shrill. "In school the little boys found me a welcome change. When they grew bored with their human girl friends they all came to Hali—she was so exotic. And you too, yes? You come to Hali when you are bored with Althea Clinger and her pretty friends. Or is your interest simply professional—making sure the visiting alien has a good time?"

"Boy, are you fucked up," Nick said, finally losing patience.

"I? Fucked up? How dare you!"

"I dare because I want to kiss you and all you can believe is that I'm using you. I'll tell you what your problem is: you hate humans but you're practically human yourself. So you wind up hating yourself, and you can't believe anyone else could feel differently."

"Oh! So now it's Terran psychology. Please, spare me your drivel."

"Look, you may not like it, but your head is just as Terran as mine—"

"Bah! That is what I say to you, bah!"

Now they reached the landing strip. Pilgrims who had stayed for supper were cleaning up their picnic spreads, folding collapsible chairs and tables, incinerating dishes and silverware. Oblivious of their audience, Nick and Hali continued the discussion.

"I am Alta-Tyberian!" she insisted. "I am blue, in case you have not noticed. My eyes are queer and my bones are hollow and I eat my babies when I am very hungry!"

"Your sarcasm doesn't impress me."

"Furthermore I find things human depressing and appalling. Your militarism, your love of technology, your squandering of resources and your rampant consumerism, your *Lifestylers*—they are worst of all! Grotesque parodies of the human form, freaks and mutants preying on human weaknesses. If you were not so confused you would understand that the one to worship is not a Lifestyler, but God—and God is all around you in every molecule of air and every atom of dust, not a thing to be assembled from recombinant DNA!"

"Miss Hasannah," Nick whispered, and his voice was suddenly urgently calm and rational, "you may or you may not be correct, but I must ask you to lower your voice because the people listening to us love the Lifestylers more than anything else in the world, and judging from the way they are looking at you, any moment now they may try and lynch you."

Silent, Hali stared at Nick. Then she looked around. Everywhere pilgrims had stopped in the midst of their cleanups and were gazing at her with undisguised hate. Not bad enough their Lex had been taken from them; now the same day to have an *alien* calling the Lifestylers mutants and freaks. . . .

"Let's go," Nick said.

Several of the pilgrims moved toward them. One held a collapsible chair which, folded, might make a first-rate bludgeon.

Nick took her arm and moved quickly past them, smiling and nodding, wishing them good evening.

Reaching the saucer, he dragged Hali up the boarding ramp. He raced to the observation bubble, seated himself at the control console and began frantically arranging the levers. Oscillating whistles emanated from the bowels of the ship.

"Sit down," Nick shouted and Hali had barely taken a seat when the ship lurched up, vertically, like a rocket. Stomachs, they felt, had been left below. Nick punched in the autopilot; only then did he dare to relax. His face was white, his hands were damp.

"Criticize anything you like about our culture," he said gently, "but don't ever, *ever*, criticize the Lifestylers. Understand?"

"I said I was sorry!" she screeched and turned and ran. He could hear the patter of her footsteps descending to the bottom deck, then the sound of her stateroom door slamming shut.

He put his elbows on the control console, cradled his head in his hands and sighed.

☒ V ☒

Nick stayed up most of the night watching the holovision reporting of Lex's murder. There were tributes to him, retrospectives of his career, interviews with his agents, managers and legal staff, even an interview with Hiram Scolpes, who looked much better than when Nick had last spoken to him.

Later Senator Harmon, in a special address to the people of Sifra Messa and the United Federation of Worlds, announced that the Lifestyler Temples would not close down! (Applause) He had arranged with Police Chief Bob Clinger for a hundred-man squadron to guard each of the remaining twenty-six temples. Meanwhile all departing spaceflights had been canceled and a planetary dragnet had been set in motion which included large cash rewards for information. While no suspects had yet been apprehended, Chief Clinger said there were many leads; he was confident of an arrest by the end of the week.

In the morning a weary, red-eyed Nick Harmon landed the ship at the temple of Sir Etherium, high atop Mt. Watson. After the welcome bump of the landing legs against the earth he went to his stateroom and slept soundly for five hours. Then he showered and dressed and knocked at Hali's door.

"I'm going to Sir Etherium's temple," he shouted, "and I'd be very happy if you came with me."

Silence.

"Only if you want to," Nick shouted. "Otherwise you can stay here."

About a minute later Hali appeared. She was wearing a robe of a thick yet lightweight mesh which fluctuated in color when it creased.

"Sleep okay?" Nick asked.

"Yes, thank you."

"Hungry?"

"No, thank you."

"Think you'll be warm enough?"

"Yes, thank you."

"Think you'll ever say anything to me besides 'Yes, thank you' and 'No, thank you'? I mean, I really don't know what you're so pissed off about, all I did was to—"

"Mr. Harmon," she interrupted, "I see no reason to prolong the arguing. We are basically incompatible. Let us be cordial shipmates for the rest of the trip, then you will go your way and I will go mine and we will never have to bother with one another again, yes? It is the best idea, I think."

"You drive me nuts," Nick said.

A chill wind whipped their clothes as they left the ship. Apparently Chief Clinger's promises had not been idle; in addition to the usual assortment of campers and buses, four gleaming black police saucers squatted at the opposite end of the landing strip. How incongruous they looked in what had been until a day ago the most crimeless and sanctified ground.

Past the strip the mountaintop was barren earth stippled with moss and a few evergreens, rocks protruding like blisters, clouds masking whatever lay in the valley beyond. The temple, a massive windowless gray cylinder, grew to awesome proportions as the slidewalk swept them nearer.

Four cops were stationed at the theater entrance with a polygraph and a sonargram stall. Every Supplicant had to undergo questioning while strapped to the polygraph, and a frisking, and a sonargramming—for concealed weapons—before they could take a seat. Nick and Hali waited on line for nearly twenty minutes. Then her turn came and, to Nick's shame, they plied her with the most bigoted sort of questions—everything short of popping eyeballs and eating children—and while she stood in the sonargram stall the cop who was operating the machine called his friends over to view the picture.

"Ever see anything like that?" the first cop asked. He wore the standard uniform, the knee-high leaping boots, the black plastic jump suit, the shiny black communications helmet and silvered visor which made him as anonymous as any mass-produced machine. His fright-stick dangled by a short cord from his utility belt; periodically he reached down to stroke it.

"Son of a bitch! What is it?"

"Looks like she's got two stomachs," offered the third.

"That's a new one on me," the second said.

When he saw what was going on Nick rushed over and explained in an urgent whisper that she was an important dignitary, a special guest of Mutagen.

"Look, sonny," the second cop said, "I don't care who she is, everybody goes through the sonargram, and aliens are particularly suspect."

"What kind of garbage is that?" Nick said. "Why are aliens particularly suspect?"

"Because they're not human," he replied logically. "If she

was a Roolik it would be something else, but I can't see what the fuck she is."

"Alta-Ty," Nick said, "and a very close friend of Senator Harmon's. I'm Senator Harmon's son—see?" Nick flashed his Mutagen ID badge. "And if you don't let her go immediately you'll all be looking for jobs tomorrow."

"The hell we will," the cop said, but his voice was uncertain. Turning his back on Nick, he shouted, "Next!"

The stall opened and Hali emerged, enraged.

"This is a very unusual situation," Nick said as they entered the theater and squeezed past more cops to get to their seats (at least sixty additional cops were stationed in key positions throughout the audience). "The cops are under a lot of political pressure, what with the elections coming up. If another murder takes place it will reflect very badly on Clinger."

Hali did not reply. Her cheeks were a mottled purple and veins in her temples throbbed. Her "beak" was clamped shut and her breath hissed strangely, as though in her anger her nonhumanness were reasserting itself, demanding recognition. Nick experienced a sudden, quite real fear that at any moment she might blow apart like a defective boiler, filling them all with brittle blue shrapnel and scalding them with the steam of her rage.

"You're right," Nick said, "this whole thing is completely inexcusable. I should have dropped you back at the hotel, it was stupid of me to—"

A man in front of them hissed for quiet. The theater darkened. Three spotlights appeared: a first picked out the podium at the front of the audience where pilgrims could voice their requests; a second—the beam of a 480× magnification projector—made a twenty-foot circle on the rear wall; the third shone stage center and within its parabola those with keen eyes could distinguish a transdimensional window no bigger than a button, suspended eight feet in the air. The magnification projector showed the window vastly enlarged; it looked identical to the window Lex had used, the shifting, trembling edges, the grayness contained within.

Seconds of silence elapsed. Then a plume of red flowed from the window like a scarf being drawn through a buttonhole. When the last of it had escaped, it formed a ball and, moving to one side of the window, hung there motionless.

The magnification screen revealed the mechanism behind the illusion, and oddly enough knowing the secret made it all the more fabulous, for the red was not a solid substance but rather a gestalt of thousands of tiny creatures (*Hymnoptera satient*) cloned from the artist who had conceived it, midwifed by Scolpes with a thousand innovative techniques, genetically modified to resemble a bee while retaining a single, semi-human consciousness.

Enlarged, he/they appeared to be flying in impossibly perfect formation, the blur of wingtips almost touching, the huge compound eyes staring in every direction, the thorax and abdomen striped with bright, bristly red fur.

Now a plume of blue seeped through the window, formed a ball and hung alongside the red one. Like the first it consisted of thousands of identical man/insects, these with blue fur on their abdomens instead of red. A third ball, a yellow one, joined the file, then a white one somewhat larger than the rest.

The four balls combined into one large ball, the three primary colors pinwheeling inward on a background of white, whirling faster and faster until they blurred. Then, in a virtuoso display of transmogrification, the sphere collapsed into a succession of objects, colors combining and recombining with dizzying speed. A housecat become a ferocious lion, a common pencil grew into a tree with thick green foliage. The magnifying screen showed the leaves to be two rows of yellow bees alternating with one row of blue, the colors combining like the dots in a newspaper photograph. The larger the object the more it tended toward translucency, the smaller, the more solid it appeared.

When the transformations threatened to become nauseating, they ceased and one ball remained, primaries pinwheeling on white. A voice came from it, rather ten thousand voices whispering in almost perfect unison, a sound slightly out of focus.

"What is matter?
Only molecules
Bound by electricity,
Insubstantial as clouds.
What does it matter?
We grow to be men

We shrink to be old
We lie in the dirt
And enrich the soil,
Soil for veggies
To feed the folks
Who have the babies
That grow to be men.
What's the matter
With transcience? All
Is Etherium,
Tell me your dream
I'll make it matter."

The audience shouted for Sir Etherium's attention. The ball took the shape of an arrow, pointed to an elderly man in the audience and beckoned, waggling like a crooked finger, for him to take the podium. He was tall and straight with white hair and nut-colored skin. His eyes were clear and blue. He spoke into the microphone:

"Sir Etherium, I'd like to see Martha, my wife, again. She died twelve years ago and hardly a night goes by when I don't fall asleep thinking about her. Maybe if I could see her one more time I could make my peace with her."

The arrow had turned back into a ball and now the ball began to spin, the colors blurring, merging into white. Faster and faster it spun, humming like a top, and then the ball broke and the whiteness assumed the form of a young woman, darkening to copper flesh, to flaxen hair.

The man turned pale.

"Martha?" he said, voice trembling.

"Yes, Joe"—ten thousand whispers in almost perfect unison.

The magnifying screen showed a section of her skin to be three rows of white bees, one row of red, with a yellow every third place.

"How is it possible . . .?" he said.

"Always wanting explanations, my Joe." She laughed. "I had to come back to tell you that the accident wasn't your fault. The other driver jumped the rail."

"But if I had turned fast enough . . ."

"No, Joe. My death was fated. Nothing you could have done would have made a difference."

"If only I could believe that."

"It's true."

He looked uncertain.

"You can't bring me back to life," she continued, "by living less yourself." Her voice grew weaker. One hand drifted away from its wrist and a section of stage showed through her abdomen.

"Don't go!" he cried and, more softly, "Not yet. So little time, it's not fair—"

"Live, Joe," she whispered. "Forget me and live. . . ."

Then there was only a ball with a three-colored pinwheel turning lazily inside. The man remained on the podium distraught, reaching with his hands toward the space she had occupied. Presently he stepped down and two priests led him back to his seat.

"How did he do that?" Hali whispered.

"He's the greatest impressionist in the galaxy."

"Yes, but how did he know the shape of her face and the sound of her voice?"

"When they go on the other side of the transdimensional window they can see a person's past."

"Really?" Her eyes opened wide. Then she remembered herself and frowned. "I think it is awful, reuniting him with his wife, then separating them again."

"Only now he's exorcised her memory, he's worked out his guilts. She won't be haunting him everywhere he goes."

"This transdimensional window . . ." Hali began, wanting to know more, but the man in front of her hissed angrily for quiet, for once again the ten thousand voices were chanting:

What is matter?
Only molecules
Bound by electricity,
Insubstantial as clouds . . ."

A woman mounted the podium, forty, short, slight and mousy. Her nose was large and the way she had her hair pulled back, it looked even larger.

"I don't want to sound discontent," she said to Sir Etherium. "I have a good life, good friends, a husband who loves me. Two wonderful children. Everything. But I've always wanted—well, it's difficult to ask. My husband says I have inner beauty and I know that's what really matters, but I still would give anything to look like one of those girls on the holovision, even for a minute. . . ."

The ball flew toward her. She put her arms over her face
for protection, which wasn't necessary; reaching her it broke
like a bubble and plumes of color moved across her body, inside her clothing, combining and recombining and finally
reaching an equilibrium, the desired effect.

When she looked again the magnifying projector had been
put in a nonmagnifying mode; the image of herself on the
rear wall was, for all intents and purposes, a mirror reflection. At first she didn't appear to know—or dare to believe—that she was looking at herself. She moved and the
glamorous woman on the screen moved. She turned and the
glamorous woman turned too, she touched herself and the
woman did the same. Identity was established.

The ten thousand parts of Sir Etherium had created a second skin, a skin like cream; new hair, rich, chestnut; new
lips, sensual; a new nose curled up, just like those of the girls
on the holovision. Her body had changed even more surprisingly: her new breasts were pushing out the top of her dress
until the seams threatened to break, and although she had
grown no taller, her legs seemed longer, her whole form more
lithe and graceful.

She began to laugh. She laughed and laughed and, leaving
the podium, skipped across the stage. She felt the hungry eyes
of the audience upon her and began to tease them, her gestures becoming more sexual and lascivious. (If new clothes
could affect the personality, then what might come of being
encompassed by Sir Etherium—one being within another,
concentric lives—or for that matter twenty thousand wings
brushing across the entire body?)

She tore open the velcro closures at the front of her dress,
easing the pressure across her chest, allowing the neck to
open wider and wider. Then, still moving in time to some inner music, she slipped the dress from her shoulders and allowed it to fall to her feet. Her breasts moved like water, her
nipples swaying and jiggling, her fingers touching the dark tri-
angle between her legs, her face transformed by unimaginable
ecstasy. A buzzing sound became more noticeable, a sound of
thousands of wings caressing her flesh, drawing the blood to
the surface so spongy tissue became hard and turgid, pouring
a maximum of stimulation into every nerve ending until the
world was blotted out by the unbearable overload and only
sensation remained, overwhelming, all-encompassing, circuit-
blowing sensation.

"Oh!" she shouted and gasped, and again: "OH! OH! OH!
OH!" Then, moaning, "Ohhh . . ."

Crumpled in a heap like a discarded robe on the dressing-
room floor, she lay there her own mousy self while Sir Etherium, an impassionate ball, revolved slowly in the air, primary
colors pinwheeling inward.

Two priests came on stage to help her on with her dress. A
third man followed, squat and barrel-chested, with beefy features. His face was scarlet, his breathing fast, his expression
outraged. As the priests tried to help her stand—her legs were
buckling under her—the man whispered, so intensely that everyone in the audience could hear: "Is that how you want the
kids to see you behaving? Well, is it? And what about me? If
you don't have any respect for yourself, at least you could
think about the way it makes me feel. . . ." And so on, and
so forth.

Hali shook her head, a faint smile playing across her lips.

"Fascinating," she whispered to Nick, "but so cruel. What
will happen to their marriage?"

"They'll have the greatest sex ever."

She thought it over. "Yes, I suppose they will."

> "What does it matter?
> We grow to be men,
> We shrink to be old,
> We lie in the . . ."

What happened next happened so quickly that many of the
people in the audience missed it completely. An eerie green
light in the shape of an aerosol can appeared in the middle of
the air and a spray of the same green light, emanating from
the can like the beacon of a lighthouse, engulfed the ball.

> "What's the matter
> With transcience? All
> Is Etherium . . ."

On the magnification screen the "bees" could be seen fal-
tering, falling from formation. Nick watched with an ache in
his heart as they tumbled to the floor like so much colorful
confetti. By the time the cops reached the stage the ball was
gone and the last of the ten thousand parts which had once
constituted Sir Etherium lay still.

"Remain in your seats," ordered an amplified voice, "do not attempt to leave . . ."

Hali bolted.

"Wait," Nick said, grabbing her wrist.

"I must get out—I'm going to be sick."

She squirmed free and ran to the aisle. Her agility and speed were remarkable; she slipped through the hands of at least ten cops. By the time Nick reached the aisle and started after her, she had vanished through the exit.

"Hold it, sonny . . ."

Nick ignored the cop and kept running. He felt the sting of a fright stick brush against his hip and the next moment he was writhing on the floor, weeping with terror. He lost control of his bladder and felt the warm urine soak his tights. He curled into a fetal ball, wishing he could roll up so small that he would vanish altogether.

"All right, sonny, don't be scared, Momma's here."

Rough hands lifted him to his feet. Holding him under the shoulders, they dragged him back to his seat. His vision was blurred with tears.

VI

He had to reach her; there was no telling what trouble she might get into alone. But the cops insisted on questioning everybody in the audience, and it was three hours before Nick was allowed to leave the theater. Then he searched the various foyers, the altar room, the box office and the nave. He asked the guide at the entrance to the Lifestyler museum (every temple had one) and the temple guards, and the ushers and priests, but most of them had been too busy during the tragedy to pay attention to aliens.

He took the glass-enclosed slidewalk back to the landing strip, adding the speed of his own legs in his impatience. He hoped to find Hali at the saucer, sitting on the steps of the boarding ramp, waiting to deliver her wrath upon him. He wouldn't mind—he wouldn't mind if she never spoke to him again just so long as she was safe.

The saucer came into sight. He leaped off the slidewalk

and ran across the landing strip, giving wide berth to the row of police saucers. With sinking heart he saw that the boarding ramp was empty. Well, perhaps she had gotten inside—he had locked the door before leaving, but conceivably Hali had watched him set the combination and memorized the numbers. So Nick hoped, not realizing the extent to which he was grasping at straws.

Inside the saucer he ran up and down the three levels calling her name. He looked everywhere, even in silly places like the electrostatic field generator access chamber. It was probably during this time, while running from room to room and silently enumerating, like a savage chanting for a favor from the gods, the ways in which he could improve his behavior if only she were returned to him, that he first realized he loved her.

After his third or fourth go-round he forced himself to stop, to sit down, to calm down and think. He was, he decided, being hysterical to no end. Really now, what harm could have come to her? Probably she had left the theater and gotten medical aid—every temple kept a doctor on call. Then when she tried to get back inside the cops would not allow it. So she went somewhere to pass the time, perhaps to one of the restaurants or relaxation rooms or gift shops in the temple annex. She would have left a message—of course! Nick shook his head at his own stupidity. The temple switchboards were intended for just that purpose. He would, no doubt, find the message waiting there.

Convinced there was no longer any urgency, Nick went down to the master bathroom and ran a shower. He peeled off his urine-soaked tights and dropped them in the launderer, then quickly switched on the holovision, the volume way up, to drown out the memory of the fright-stick. The shower was pure pleasure, the needles of water pounding his face, the heat loosening his muscles; and finally being rid of the urine smell!

Not surprisingly, regular broadcasts had been suspended for special coverage of the murder. The circumstances of Sir Etherium's death, the announcer said, left no doubt that the same person was responsible for both Lifestyler deaths. And—wait a minute, a special bulletin had just been handed him—Chief Clinger was proud to announce that the murderer had been apprehended.

"Yahooo!" Nick screamed and threw the soap in the air.

"Brain-wipe the bastard!" he added, carried away with enthusiasm and perhaps a trace of blood lust.

The murderer, the announcer continued, was an alien who had been touring Sifra Messa as a guest of Mutagen Laboratories. She had been apprehended while fleeing Sir Etherium's temple immediately following the murder. Her name was . . .

But by then Nick was out of the shower, drying himself, rushing so to get dressed that he put the clean pair of tights on backward.

✺ VII ✺

Of the four police saucers on the landing strip, one was unusually busy. A double guard stood duty outside and an assortment of cops, journalists and delivery boys lugging cartons of stimu-caff and quik-snax paraded up and down the boarding ramp. Nick fast-talked his way inside, flashing his Mutagen badge and claiming to be part of the company security force.

The police saucers were divided into three levels like his own craft, but instead of a few spacious rooms, each floor was honeycombed with cells barely large enough to sleep a man. Nick passed a cell where a cop was dictyping forms and another where five journalists, squeezed tight as plutonium atoms, were radioing reports to their home offices. Two more cells had been converted to laboratories, and in a third cops and journalists were playing heptacard draw for high stakes. The joint smoke, a mixture of alpha and dimethyl tryptamine crystals, which smelled like dirty socks, was so thick Nick feared he would pass out before he reached the lifter.

The sergeant who stopped him at the second level wasn't as obliging as the one outside.

"Nobody sees the alien," he said, and that was that.

Nick insisted on speaking to the next in command. He pestered until the sergeant grumbled into an intercom. A few minutes later another cop appeared, this one with lieutenant bars on the breast of his black plastic suit.

He looked Nick over and said, with obvious enjoyment, "It's the one who made pee-pee."

His eyes were covered by the standard silver visor. What showed of his face was a gray stubble, pale lips and teeth that overlapped like a badly made fence; Nick couldn't say if he was the one who had touched him with the fright-stick.

"You're a friend of the alien's," the lieutenant continued. "Am I right? Harmon, the senator's kid."

"That's right, and she's *not* the murderer. I know, I've been with her day and night for the last three days."

"Day and night?" The lieutenant's lips curled. "What's that alien pussy like? I always wanted to get me a piece." As he spoke he rubbed the base of his fright-stick more and more rapidly.

Nick took deep breaths, determined to remain calm. "Can I please see her?"

"Sure," the lieutenant said, "sure you can. Right this way."

Hali looked up when Nick entered the room. Then she looked away. She was sitting in a reasonably comfortable chair, no visible bruises or other signs of mistreatment, no bindings or gags or manacles, although two cops watched her with raised nerve guns and two others, similarly armed, stood at the door. A technician knelt next to her, fiddling with a black box on rollers from which dozens of wires connected to Hali's wrists and chest and temples.

Nick stared at it with horror. "If you've brain-wiped her, I swear I'll—"

"Relax, it's a special polygraph we use on aliens. But it's no damn good on this, this . . ."

"Alta-Tyberian."

"Whatever. She's got voluntary metabolic control. We can't get an operational standard."

"You're wasting your time," Nick insisted. "She's from the quietest, most peace-loving civilization in the galaxy. They *eat flowers!*" He lowered his voice. "And if you don't release her right away you're going to be responsible for an extremely embarrassing interstellar incident. Look, if you don't believe me, call Senator Harmon. He'll straighten this out."

The lieutenant thought it over. Then he nodded to one of the cops. "Get me an outside line with a holocube interface."

Nick gave them the number, and soon the senator could be seen within the milky depths of his life-preserver jar.

"Thank God you're there," Nick said. "They're holding Ms. Hasannah as the Lifestyler murderer."

"I know," the senator said. "I've been watching the bulletins."

"Well, aren't you going to do something?"

"Who's in charge there?"

"Lieutenant-Detective Addington, sir," the lieutenant said, stepping smartly into the field of view.

"Addington," the senator said, "do you have sufficient evidence to hold the alien?"

"I believe we do, sir. She was one of seven who were present at both murders, and of the seven she was the only alien. Immediately after Sir Etherium's murder she tried to flee the temple and evaded cops who wished to detain her for questioning. That's grounds right there. Furthermore . . ." He stopped to shuffle through some cassettes on the table, found one and snapped it into a player. He handed the player to one of the cops, saying, "Half holocube interface." Then, to Senator Harmon, "Take a look at this."

The cop plugged the player module into the holocube base. As he turned the dials the senator's head shrank until it filled only half the cube; the other half was taken up by a recording of a pudgy, balding fifty-five-year-old man with sweat beaded across his forehead and upper lip. He was looking off to the left, presumably at the interrogator.

A voice off screen said, "So you saw the aforementioned alien the evening of the murder of Lex Largesse?"

"Yes I did," the pudgy man said. "It was on the Great Plain of Crick, right near the temple, at 22:00 hours. I remember 'cause I'd just put the twins to sleep in the camper. That's their regular bedtime, 22:00. Anyway, I was taking the night air when I saw them coming across the landing strip, her and a human male. Sounded to me like they were fighting."

"And can you tell us," the off-screen interrogator said, "what they were fighting about?"

"First she was screaming about how she was Alpha Superior or something and how she hated everything human."

"Did she mention Lifestylers?"

"She did. To the best of my recollection she said, 'Your Lifestylers are the worst of all. They're freaks and mutants. They take advantage of human beings.' "

"That's enough," Lieutenant Addington said.

The cop pulled the player module out of the base and the senator swelled to fill the cube.

"Wait a minute," Nick said, before anyone could speak. "What about"—he thought furiously—"what about the psych field amp? Scolpes said nobody could work it."

"Only people with strong psi powers," Addington said. "And she's got them."

"Prove it."

"I've got a tape of a nurse at Averyville General who says she saw the alien heal some burns on your back by running her fingers across them. If that isn't psi powers, I don't know what is."

Nick had forgotten about that and regretted having brought attention to it.

"But she was with me during the murders. Wouldn't I have seen her working it?"

"Not necessarily. She could have used the amp before the murders took place. From what I hear, you imagine something happening in the future and the damned machine makes it happen in the future."

"She didn't kill them," Nick said. "I *know* she didn't kill them." He turned to the holocube. "Pop, do something, don't let them take her away."

"I don't see what I can do," the senator said, his voice as calm as always. "Lieutenant Addington seems to have more than sufficient evidence. We cannot countermand the law whenever it displeases us and expect it to protect us the rest of the time.

"I regret to say," he continued, "that I anticipated something of this nature. Apparently the Alta-Tys are not the friends they would have us think. But this is not your problem, Nicholas. You are no longer responsible for Ms. Hasannah. Mutagen has decided to discontinue work on the Alta-Ty problem—"

Hali, who had been sitting silently through all this, her head bent forward on her long slender neck like a blossom on a drooping stem, suddenly rose from her chair crying, "You must not abandon us, you are the only ones we can turn to. Do what you like with me, but save my people!"

The cops closed in on either side of her; they lowered her to the chair, and one of them brought her a glass of water.

"We'll continue this conversation later," the senator said. His head faded from the cube.

Nick just stood there feeling stupid and awkward. Lieutenant Addington was smiling at him with his crooked teeth. Those teeth. Nick wanted to knock them down his throat. Instead he turned around and left.

VIII

When Nick returned to his saucer the message light was blinking: Morgan Grim wanted him to call back as soon as possible. Nick tapped out Morgan's code and seconds later that redhead's image was inside the holocube.

"Nicky, I hate to cut short your vacation but we need you at the office. Fly back tonight—or in the morning if you're too beat."

"What about Hali? I can't leave her."

"You can and you will. We don't owe the Alta-Tys a damn thing. Our boys have been busting their balls over this project for a week and a half and all we've got in compensation is two dead Lifestylers."

"But she didn't do it!"

"That's for the courts to decide. Meanwhile we've got a job to do. The paperwork's four feet high on your desk."

"What if I don't come?" Nick blurted out, before he could think about what he was saying.

Morgan didn't hesitate a second. "First I have Central Power cut off energy transmissions to your saucer. Then I notify the Bank of the Cosmos that you're no longer working for Mutagen and they stop your credit lines. Want more? You look for a new job, but you can't go back to Mutagen. So instead you try the snack bar or maybe driving a cab. Naturally you can't afford to stay in the club; you have to give up rocket polo and—Nicky, Nicky, Nicky, why are we talking this nonsense? You're a sensible young man with a full life and a promising career. You're not going to give it all up for some alien woman you've hardly known two weeks!"

"Yeah." Nick laughed. "I don't know what I could have been thinking."

PART IV

Life Back to Normal

I

Four feet of papers had been a slight exaggeration; still, enough work had accumulated to keep Nick very busy. Yet somehow he could not concentrate. He would read a simple technical paper three times through without comprehending a word; he would listen to Morgan for a half hour and recall nothing of what had been said.

Hiram Scolpes was delighted when Nick stopped by his office at lunch. The old man looked tired. A loss of weight had caused his face to craze with wrinkles like a balloon which had lost some air, yet his gray eyes seemed even wiser and more compassionate than before the tragedies.

He cleared the clutter off a chair and offered it to Nick. He took a minute to call downstairs for stimu-caff and quik-snax before settling into an ancient, beloved easy chair and beginning to talk.

"I've been giving some thought to these murders. It seems to me I was upset because I saw Lex and Etherium as outgrowths of myself. Extensions of my ego. When I heard of their deaths it was as though I'd lost a hand. Nicholas, we draw lessons to ourselves, and the lesson is that simply because we can shape the flesh, we must not come to believe that we are gods. Hubris, the Greeks called it. Insolence, overbearing pride. I thought Lex and Etherium were my creations. My petty ego blinded me to the truth. *Recombinant*—that's the key; we do not create, we recombine. Only He creates."

"He?"

"Anyone who works with a mechanism as intricate and elegant as DNA comes to believe in a God of one sort or another. The real tragedy," Scolpes continued, "is your lovely Alta-Tyberian friend. I will recover and new Lifestylers will be produced, but she and her people appear to be bound for oblivion. And we had almost cracked their genetic code, that's what's so frustrating. Another two weeks . . ."

"She didn't do it."

"Of course she didn't. What conceivable reason would she

81

have? That she hates humans? My dear Nicholas, there are times when *I* hate humans, but I don't go out and murder a Lifestyler. My guess is that Chief Clinger has made her the sacrificial lamb."

"Would he do that?"

Scolpes shrugged. "It's happened before. Remember your Terran history. Late twentieth century. Every time an important, beloved figure was assassinated the police found some hapless drifter and pinned the charges on him. It satisfied the public and earned the cops commendations. And the real murderers—or so it was revealed decades later when certain files came to light—the real murderers were always a well-organized political body. A conspiracy."

"You mean with the Kennedys and Samuelson and Martin Luther King? Yeah, I guess it's possible." Nick's gaze wandered. "I should have stayed with her," he murmured.

"Pardon me?"

"Nothing," Nick said, but Scolpes knew what he was referring to.

"What good could you have done? Some pointless act of heroism ending with a buzz of nerve guns and you reduced to a zombie for the rest of your life? No, Nicholas, the police are too powerful, the government too far removed from the people. That is the price we pay for our years of political indifference. Now put it out of your mind before it becomes an obsession. I've seen men ruined by such things."

❖ II ❖

Nick left work early that day. He changed into his best cape, the turquoise one with the Lifestylers embroidered on it, and proceeded to the club. First he went to the member's infirmary and had an injection of hypothalamus stimulant to counter his depression, which was growing worse by the moment. Next he visited the "Smoking Room" and consumed, down to the roach, four joints of old-fashioned tetra-hydracannabinal to fill the cracks left by the injection. While rolling a fifth his old buddies Tom Sultan and Larry "Crackin' Heads" Parsee appeared, and told him they had

missed his face on the rocket-polo court. They offered Nick a
nasal inhaler containing a solution of tri-methoxy-amphet-
amine and he accepted, hoping it would restore his flagging
energies. Indeed, the liquid exploded against the delicate
membranes inside his nose, filling his head with sunbursts and
roman candles. And still, despite all this chemical hanky-
panky, he felt that he did not much wish to continue living.

As he staggered into the dining room, the floor undulating
beneath his feet, the ceiling fixtures turning into toe-hanging
pterodactyls waiting to sink their stiletto beaks into the first
juicy twenty-fourth-century Neanderthal to happen along,
somebody called. The name sounded curiously familiar; Nick
was so stoned it took him five seconds to realize it was his
own. He turned to see Althea Clinger and her two best
friends, Aynn Draper, a tall, quiet girl with straight black
hair and a funereal air, and Dorce Ramonn, who was
bosomy and giggled a lot. None of them was past eighteen.

"Could this be clean-living Nick Harmon," Althea asked in
mock astonishment, "who only has a social smoke now and
then?"

"None other," he mumbled. He eyed the ceiling fixtures
warily.

This reduced the three girls to helpless laughter.

"You've been such a bad boy," Althea scolded. "You
haven't called in weeks."

"He's been busy," Dorce explained, "in the Department of
Alien Affairs."

"Was she better than me?" Althea asked.

"Did she have anything special," Dorce wanted to know,
"down there?"

"Hey," Nick said, shaking his head. "I don't want to talk
about it." He looked at Althea and looked away. If he stared
too long her face turned into a death mask. He felt a cold
sweat on the back of his neck, and suspected that men in
black capes were hiding in the shadows, waiting for him.

"Oh come on, don't be an old stuffy. Did she teach you
any—"

"*I said I don't want to talk about it!*"

"Pardon me for breathing."

"I'm sorry, Althea, it's the dope. I'm feeling . . . *paranoid.*"

"You sure are. What you need is three of the best lovers on
Sifra Messa to smooth you out. Am I right, Dorce?"

"Absolutely."

"Aynn?"

The tall girl smiled shyly and nodded.

They commandeered Nick, maneuvered him out of the club house, through the orchid garden and across the rolling lawns to the club "Motel," a two-story prestressed-concrete cube designed according to Terran tradition.

Inside, the robo-clerk, upon whose face some wit had pasted a paper mustache, took a key off a hook and led them down the hall.

The room he showed them was dominated by a massive satin-sheeted waterbed. The ceiling and walls were mirrored and the floor was covered with Altairan carpetgrass. Among the many toys and conveniences were a sunken whirlpool bath, a cage of fuzzy little lickers, a small fridge of intoxicants and a larger chest of sexual accessories including graduated cock rings, brass ben-was, condoms of every shape and size, ribbed, nibbed, knobbed and nubbled, dildos and vibrators, a stimusonic jacket for those who took too long and an electroanesthetic girdle for those who came too soon.

In minutes the girls were naked and sloshing on the waterbed.

"Nicky," Althea called, "planning to join us?"

He was gazing out the window, fully clothed. Slowly he turned.

"Huh?"

The waterbed rocked with laughter. What could have been funnier—or more adorable—than this big, strapping young man drugged helpless as a baby?

They pulled him over to the bed and undressed him. At first his penis was as disinterested as the rest of him, but Althea found a pack of Aphro-Deeza pheramone poppers in the fridge and one of them, cracked under his nose, did the trick. While Nick lay there thinking other things, she squatted above him and shimmied down onto his rigid organ, uttering small groans of pleasure. Dorce wedged her head between his legs, taking his balls into her mouth while reaching around to caress Althea's tummy and pinch her hard nipples. Aynn occupied herself with Dorce's cunt, and Nick, moved from his lethargy by social convention and the desire for symmetry, began to suck, halfheartedly, on Aynn's big toe.

Without feeling, without love, which is, in the case of intercourse, *content*, variations of form are quickly exhausted;

hence the boredom, the desperate quest for novelty which earmarked the sexual exploits of Averyville's young folk, who strove to find in the latter what the former would not yield. And so, twenty-three orgasms later (a total count), ennui crept in and Althea, disregarding Nick's wishes, again brought up a topic which fascinated her beyond reason.

"What was she like? The alien, I mean. Did she eat living flesh or pop her eyeballs or anything like that?"

Nick recalled the cool touch of Hali's fingertips the day she healed his wounds, the feel of her pliant beak the night they kissed. He got up and started to dress.

"Don't leave, Nicky," they called. "Please don't go!"

"I must have been crazy," he muttered, pulling on his tights. "I thought I could come back to this life. . . . I can't ever come back."

"Please stay," Althea whimpered. "We'll do anything."

Her friends echoed the sentiment.

Nick laughed and shook his head. "There's nothing you can do for me."

While buttoning his codpiece he remembered Scolpes' words about assassination in the late twentieth century. What other techniques had been used to gain leverage against powerful police and inaccessible governments?

He had an idea. A funny look came into his eyes and a smile began at the corners of his mouth. At that moment life returned to him; the drug haze lifted from his mind and his perceptions became razor-sharp.

"Anything?"

"Anything!"

"All right, girls," he said, sitting down at the edge of the bed, "if you *really* mean it—then I'll show you how I made love to the alien."

They laughed and clapped their hands in anticipation. Alien sex was the greatest novelty of all.

"But I'm warning you, it's pretty bizarre. Sure you want to go through with it?"

They did. Unquestionably.

"First you'll have to get me some props." Nick rattled off a list.

"A nerve gun?" Althea asked, raising her eyebrows. "What's that for?"

"You'll see."

"I don't know where I could get a nerve gun this time of night. Anyway, you need a license and—"

"You're right," Nick said. "We'd better forget the whole thing."

"Wait—Daddy keeps one in the night table. I might be able to . . ."

An hour later they reconvened at the motel. Quiet, retiring Aynn brought her sexual-bondage set, as instructed, a suitcase full of ball gags, handcuffs, leg irons and an assortment of real leather belts for securing the body in a variety of positions.

Dorce wouldn't say where she had obtained a GE chair at this hour of night, but Nick had a hunch she had stolen it out from under some unfortunate cripple. Petty thievery was one of the girls' favorite diversions.

And Althea, good old Althea, showed up with the nerve gun. Nick hefted its cool oily weight in his hand and kissed her approvingly on the forehead.

"My folks were asleep," she confessed. "I tiptoed in and took it." She laughed. "If Daddy finds out he'll dock me for a week."

"Nice going," Nick said. "Now who wants to be first?"

"Me," they all shouted, "oh me, Nicky, please, me, me, me."

"Althea," Nick said, like a pagan priest picking the sacrificial virgin.

Althea stripped to her underwear, a cross-bra and a culotte of late-twenty-first-century vintage, now considered "erotic antiques." The black silk was striking against her blond hair. She made herself comfortable in the GE chair while Aynn, the expert on bondage, belted her firmly in place. Slim ankles chained to chair legs, arms pulled back and handcuffed behind, a strap cutting into her small tummy and a ball gag plugging her mouth.

Nick told Aynn and Dorce to wait outside. When they accused him of favoritism, he explained that watching would spoil the surprise. He told them to come back in an hour and, resigned, they trotted off to the snack bar.

Now Nick and Althea were alone. He circled her GE chair, inspecting the bonds. "Pretty snug?"

"Uh-huh."

"Think you could wriggle out?"

"Unh-unh."

"I'm sorry I have to do this," he began, pacing the room. "It's not like I have anything against you."

"Huuunh?"

He sat down on the bed, very close to her, and continued, looking deep into her eyes.

"I've never considered myself a principled person. I always thought that if I found myself in a situation where I had to choose between my beliefs and my personal comfort, comfort would win hands down. But when you think about these things in the abstract, you don't understand that it's not a conscious decision; when it really happens, it's not so much a case of what you want to do as what you *have* to do."

"Whaa yaa awahhh?"

"And to do what I have to do, I need your help. Things may get pretty hairy, but I promise you, Althea, I won't hurt you unless I absolutely have to."

"Huh? Ih-hee, ah owah ahh?!!"

"Shh—save your strength."

He interfaced the holocube with the phone, and the robo-clerk appeared, sporting its mustache.

"Get me," Nick said, "394-674-340."

"Hunh! hunh! hunh!" She shook her head frantically.

The circuit was connected and static snow gave way to a slow play of kaleidoscopic patterns. A voice said, "I'm sorry, Police Chief Clinger and his wife have already gone to bed. Please call again in the morning. If this is an emergency, remain on the line; in forty-five seconds an alarm will ring and your call will be answered."

The forty-five seconds seemed like an hour; then he heard a click and a groggy voice (still no visual):

"Yeah?"

"Chief Clinger? This is Nick Harmon. I've got something to show you."

"What is this, a joke? It's the middle of the night."

"Definitely not a joke, sir."

"Call me in the morning."

"Before you disconnect, look in your night table—I think you'll find your nerve gun missing."

A grunt, a mutter, a sliding of a drawer. An exclamation.

"Yeah, it's missing. What's it got to do with you, Harmon?"

"If you'll turn on the visual, you'll see."

A sigh. Clinger's head appeared within the cube, a pale, horsy face with dark rings under the eyes. He slept with a hair press; he'd neglected to take it off before answering the phone. Nick repressed an urge to giggle.

"All right," Clinger grumbled, "what is it?"

Nick slid Althea into view. He held the nerve gun to her temple and said, "If you don't do exactly as I say, I'll burn her out."

Chief Clinger's mouth fell open. Funny noises came from deep in his throat. Regaining his speech, he said, "If this is a joke . . ."

"Try me and see," Nick said coolly.

"Take that damn thing out of her mouth and let her speak to me!"

Nick obliged. Althea gasped and coughed and spit defiantly in his face.

"Are you all right, baby?" Chief Clinger asked.

"He forced me into this, he made me steal the gun. I didn't want to do it but he forced me. Don't let him hurt me, Daddy . . ."

Nick eased the ball gag back in her mouth.

Now Clinger's tone changed. "Harmon, how can you do this to me? I'm nobody, a minor functionary on an out-of-the-way planet. What have I got? Nothing but my little girl. If anything happens to her, I'll—"

"Do what I say, Mr. Clinger, and nothing will happen to her."

"Robert," a sleepy woman's voice demanded, "who are you talking to at this hour?"

Chief Clinger scowled to his left. "Go back to sleep, Abby."

The face of a plump, white-haired woman peered curiously into the corner of the cube. Her eyes took in Nick, her daughter, the nerve gun; the next moment she was hysterical and her husband was ordering her to shut up.

"Now listen to me," Nick said, when she had finally been quieted down and dispatched to the kitchen for stimu-caff. "Hali Hasannah did not murder Sir Etherium or Lex Largesse. Somebody else did—and they did it in order to silence them. I don't know what they had to say that was so important, but I'll bet some of the other Lifestylers do. So here's my first demand: I want an hour alone with as many of the Lifestylers as you can contact tonight."

"That means an hour by yourself, Harmon. After the second murder the Lifestylers all went over to the other side. They've sealed the transdimensional windows and cut off communications. They're scared for their lives, and I don't blame them."

"Shit," Nick said. "Let me think for a minute. Scolpes. That's it, I want to see Scolpes. Call him up right now and tell him to meet me at his laboratory in half an hour. Then I want a MagLev wagon with a robo-chauff to take Althea and me to Mutagen. And I'm warning you, Mr. Clinger, try anything and I'll brain-wipe your daughter."

"We'd snuff you so fast, Harmon . . ."

Oddly enough, the threat didn't bother him. If he did nothing to save Hali, his life was worthless; if he died saving her, his life took on immense value. And if he succeeded in saving her, well, that would be best of all. He realized with surprise what men sometimes learn in times of crises; that dying nobly can be preferable to living inanely.

❖ III ❖

None of his crimes thus far caused Nick the chagrin he experienced entering Scolpes' lab at Mutagen without a sterile suit (donning one would have left him defenseless). Actually the sterile suits were part of a multi-redundant system and he knew it would do no harm to go without it this once. But the habit had been so deeply ingrained, he felt as though he were appearing naked in public.

Scolpes gazed in amazement from within the fishbowl helmet of his own suit as Nick slid in Althea, all pink skin and black undies, leather belts and shiny chrome handcuffs. She became doubly incongruous juxtaposed against the cool photon microscopes, the impassive computer consoles.

"What in the world?"

"I've taken her hostage," Nick explained, "until I can clear Hali of this crime."

"You're mad."

"Yeah, maybe. But I feel great."

"Nicholas, you cannot jeopardize this girl's life. She's not responsible for what happened to Ms. Hasannah. And think of the anguish you must be causing her parents."

"I have to do what I have to do," Nick said, "and I need your help."

Nick held his breath while the old man thought it over. Presently Scolpes nodded.

"What can I do?"

"I want you to alter me with transdimensional replicon. The Lifestylers have holed up on the other side, and that's the only way I'm going to get to talk to them."

"Do you know what that entails?" Scolpes voice took on new gravity. "It's more than a simple vaccination. The entire chemistry of the brain is altered, and after that's done it takes time to learn to activate the dormant sections of the cerebrum—rather like learning to wiggle one's ears. You may be able to open the transdimensional window immediately; then again it may take you weeks or months. There will be unpleasant side effects, headaches, swelling of the glands. Skin rashes. When and if you do reach the other side, laws of motion will be reversed: objects will grow more distant as you move toward them and closer when you move away. Left and right are transposed and time becomes a simultaneity. The senses are in constant confusion. *If you lose sight of the window from which you entered, you may never find your way back to the real world.* Are you sure you want this? Does the alien mean so much to you?"

"It's not just her," Nick said. "I've got a feeling a lot more is at stake."

Scolpes kept arguing. His affection for Nick, his unwillingness to jeopardize the young man's life for what he thought a futile cause, was obvious; but Nick was adamant. Eventually Scolpes dialed for a robo-courier to bring up a vial of transdimensional replicon from one of the coldroom "libraries," and also some special growth factor to speed the change.

They waited uneasily. Ten minutes later a bell chimed and a blue light flashed on the door control.

"Identify yourself," Scolpes called.

A sequence of integers appeared below the light. Scolpes relaxed slightly.

"That's the code for our robo-courier," he told Nick. *"Admit to shower."*

A yellow light flashed alongside the blue, signaling that the radiation shower was in use.

"Admit to room."

A green light flashed, the third in the row, and the door began to open. Involuntarily, Nick swung the barrel of the nerve gun away from Althea's head and aimed it at the opening.

A fat silver robot rolled in carrying a tray of vials.

Nick chuckled nervously and returned the gun to her head. The weight of it was making his wrist ache.

"Put them over here," Scolpes ordered. The robot lowered the tray to one of the counters.

"That will be all," Scolpes said.

The robot turned and advanced toward Nick.

"I said, *that will be all!*"

Before Nick could move, one hydraulic arm shot out; pincer fingers gripped the gun and turned it so the barrel faced the ceiling. Nick immediately smashed the robot's faceplate with his fist, reached inside and yanked out the photoelectric scanning device which functioned as eyes, immobilizing the machine. While he was trying to pry the gun out of its steel grip, he noticed that the door was opening again, and he caught a glimpse of shiny black police uniforms outside.

"Scolpes," he shouted, "the door . . ."

But Scolpes had already noticed it. He sprinted across the room and yanked a large red lever on the wall marked "Emergency Containment."

A metal panel slammed over the half-open door and three more fell like guillotine blades across the windows. Powerful ventilating fans came to life, sucking the "contaminated" air from the room and treating it with ultraviolet radiation. Things began to smell of ozone.

Scolpes collapsed in a chair, holding his hand over his heart. "Oh my," he murmured, "oh my . . ."

Once Nick had succeeded in prying the gun from the robot's fingers with a screwdriver, he ran to Scolpes' side.

"Are you okay, Doc?"

His breathing was labored. "Help me with this," he gasped.

Nick unfastened the clasps and lifted the helmet off Scolpes' head. The old man took a blue tablet out of his sterile suit pocket, squeezed it between his fingers—it made a cracking sound—and placed it under his tongue. In a minute his breath returned to normal and a protuberant vein in his forehead stopped throbbing.

For a time they both sat there recovering their wits. The phone chimed and Nick answered it. Chief Clinger filled the cube.

"Harmon," he said quickly, "a couple of my boys were overzealous. They didn't tell me they were going to try this stupid stunt; I never would have permitted it—do you understand?"

"Sure."

"But now I'm here, I'm right here in the hall and I'm personally making sure it won't happen again. Althea—she's all right? You didn't . . . ?"

"I didn't. But next time I will. And I've got Scolpes tied up, too," Nick improvised, glancing over his shoulder to make sure Scolpes was out of camera range. "If I have to wipe Althea he'll take her place."

"No, no, Harmon, that's the last thing we want. No violence. We'll do whatever you say."

"Good. My second demand: I want a small, fast MHD saucer delivered to the garden outside this post—and you better get me one with storage cells. I don't want to be drawing off the power satellites. Make sure it has SAB Standard instrumentation. And make sure Ms. Hasannah is in the back seat."

"Harmon, we can't! She's a prisoner of the Federation. She's already been transferred to the maximum-security facilities at Mendeltown and . . ."

As Clinger spoke, Nick went over to a cage of white rats. Scolpes had grown fond of the creatures during student days and kept them as pets, along with all the other clutter. Loving animals as he did, he never experimented on them; and Nick, who had had many of his values formed by this gentle old man, held them in similar regard. However, if life was the currency of the universe, the sacrifice of one small creature to save a few large ones might be a bargain.

He removed a rat from the cage and dangled it by the tail in front of the holocube. Clinger kept right on talking:

" . . . might take days to get her released. We couldn't do it without a presidential pardon, and the president is a hard man to reach. After all, I'm just a minor functionary on an out-of-the-way planet, I'd have to apply for an audience and . . ."

The rat wriggled its nose and made cheeping noises. It was so beautiful in its soft whiteness, with its dainty pink feet. Nick silently asked forgiveness for what he was about to do.

". . . to be reasonable, Harmon! We'll do anything we can, but we can't do the impossible. The alien will get a fair trial and a . . ."

Nick pointed the nerve gun and squeezed the trigger. The rat squealed and stiffened, then it hung limp. Chief Clinger never finished his sentence; he watched dumbfounded as Nick placed the creature on the counter. It stood there staring stupidly ahead. It could still eat and excrete, and perform a few of the simplest motor functions (of course on humans the effect was far more dramatic). Still without a word, Nick went over to Althea and pressed the wand to her temple.

"All right, Harmon," Clinger cried. "We'll get her to you—I don't know how, but we'll get her to you."

While they waited, Scolpes injected Nick with transdimensional replicon.

✿ IV ✿

Floodlights turned the garden into harsh patterns of black and white, and glared from the silvery surface of the saucer which had landed minutes before. It was similar to the company ship Nick had flown, only smaller, a scant sixteen feet in diameter, with one deck. On either side of the observation bubble a hydrogen booster was elevated on a streamlined fin. Nick tried to see within the bubble, but the floodlights were too much competition.

Around the saucer a broad circle had been cordoned off. Journalists with camera crews and crowds of curious onlookers were straining for a view. Nick recognized Dorce and Aynn, looking as though they'd been horribly cheated, and Mrs. Clinger crying into a handkerchief, and Chief Clinger directing operations with a walkie-talkie.

As he entered the floodlighted area, pushing his hostage

roughly in front of him—he had untied her from the chair, leaving only handcuffs and ball gag—split-beam holocameras focused on them and the crowd began to buzz. He felt like a rare species on exhibit at the zoo.

He moved quickly now, hugging Althea to him so any marksman might have difficulty picking him off. He hurried her up the boarding ramp and shoved her through the hatch. The dark interior made him even more uncomfortable. Shadows and alcoves, lockers and access hatches, too many places to hide. He opaqued the bubble, depriving the cops outside of an easy target, and then turned on the lights.

There was Hali.

"Hello," Nick said.

"Hello."

"How are you?"

"I am well." She smiled. It sounded like conversation over tea. "And you?"

Nick shrugged. "No complaints." Then he smiled too, but only for a minute; next thing he was racing around again, tying Althea to one of the couches, arming himself with nerve gun and flashlight and inspecting the ship, inch by inch. Fifteen minutes later, satisfied that the craft was more or less what he had requested, and that it concealed neither cops nor devices of sabotage, he raised it into the air.

✿ V ✿

Cruising low over Darwin's Desert in the relatively uninhabited northeast sector of the continent, Nick spied a small garage like a pimple in the middle of an otherwise smooth face. He had Hali buckle into her couch—they were maneuvering at close to Mach 2—and began a descent.

Despite all his precautions, he was certain that a bug had been planted aboard the ship. Since it might be a submicrominiaturized piece of nanocircuitry (long organo metallic molecules used as circuit elements) no bigger than a dust mote, his chances of locating it without special equipment were almost nil. However, if the garage was at all well equipped, they would have a pan-frequency signal tracer, with which he could root out a bug, no matter how small its size.

Radar revealed that Chief Clinger was keeping his word; they were not being pursued, at least not yet. Nick could certainly spare a few minutes for this precaution.

He lowered the saucer until it hovered only inches above the pale sand and taxied to the entrance. From the ground the garage appeared to be a collapsible Fullerdome hangar joined with three module-shax, a cheap, mass-produced housing system in which rooms could be added at whim.

Before leaving he made Hali promise to keep an eye on Althea.

"I truly must be ninety percent human," she said, accepting the gun as though it were some slimy lizard. "No Alta-Ty would ever do such a thing."

"Just be human until we're out of danger. Then you can be anything you want."

He climbed down from the saucer and slogged through the sand. As he approached the entrance, electronic music poured over him like a thick sweet syrup, one of those radio stations the kids played.

> "I'm savin' all my money for a geno-engineer,
> Tell you what I want him to fix,
> Turn my poor ears from flesh to wax
> So I won't go fallin' for your tricks."

His steps echoed across the concrete floor of the dome. The yellow plastic roof was semi-transparent, and sunlight bathed the strange machine which stood in front of him in a golden radiance.

It was animal-like, with silk skin stretched across bones of wood, with two pairs of wings and a tail, with clumsy balloon tires for feet. A man in bright-orange overalls was working inside the cockpit, and a woman, similarly dressed, had her head under the engine cowling. Only her trim rear protruded, wiggling in time to the music.

> "I'm savin' up my money for a geno-engineer,
> Tell you what I want him to change,
> Turn my poor eyes from flesh to glass
> So the sight of you won't drive me insane!"

Nick cleared his throat and the sound echoed all around. The girl pulled her head out from under the cowling and faced him. She was no more than sixteen, with acne around her nose and big blue eyes filled with wonder. Her hair was thickly greased and coiffed in the shape of a cube.

Of course, Nick thought. *Greaseheads.* They were called that because they greased their hair, but also because they had grease on their minds—that is to say, they worshipped machines. Nick didn't fully understand their creed, something about finding enlightenment by immersing oneself in the maintenance of machinery, something like that. They even had their own Lifestyler, titled, simply enough, Mr. Machine, an assembly of fleshy gears and levers, of entrails pulled into pulleys, of organs turned into worm gears. But these socio-religious fads came and went like the seasons, and Nick couldn't believe that anything so transient could mirror, even in part, eternity.

> "I'm savin' all my money for a geno-engineer,
> Tell you what I want him to do,
> Turn my poor heart from flesh to stone,
> So you won't go breakin' it in two!"

"Joe," she called, rapping her knuckles on the windshield, "we've got a visitor."

The man climbed out of the cockpit, grinning. He was Nick's age, but smaller and skinnier, with a look of surpassing gentleness and a way of chewing his gum that reminded Nick of a cow chewing cud. His hair too was greased and pressed into a cube. He trotted to Nick, wiping his hands on his overalls.

"Welcome, friend."

"Hi," Nick said. "I've got an MHD saucer parked outside—I'm having some trouble with her and I was wondering if you had a pan-frequency signal tracer I could use for a couple of minutes."

"Sorry. All I've worked on for the last couple of years is *Cynthia* here"—he patted the machine affectionately—"and she's so simple I wouldn't have any use for a tracer."

"What is it?" Nick said. "An airplane?"

"That's right. Internal combustion. Propeller pushes the air back, wings lift it up, tail stabilizes and steers. Just like they used on classical Terra, but I made some improvements of my own."

"Improve the machine," the girl said—Wanda was her name—"improve the self."

"Computerized most of the controls," he continued, "installed Standard SAB instrumentation, modified the engine to run on hydrogen."

"And he did it all by hand," Wanda said proudly. "Took him three years."

"It's beautiful," Nick said, "but I'd better be going. Thanks anyway."

"Hey, wait a minute," Joe said. "Tell me what you need the tracer for. Maybe I can improvise something."

The song had ended, and now a news broadcast took its place, the announcer's voice rising to fill the silence:

" . . . escaped with the alien and a hostage in a Class A MHD saucer . . . are expected to be somewhere in Darwin's Desert . . . Black hair, brown eyes, six feet, two inches, muscular build . . . Harmon is armed and may be dangerous . . ."

Wanda and Joe looked at each other, and then they looked at Nick.

"Are you him?" Joe said. The only emotion in his voice was curiosity.

Nick hesitated. He trusted his instincts about people, and this greasehead seemed totally guileless. Furthermore, greaseheads were loners, notoriously opposed to bureaucracy of any sort. He'd chance it.

"I am."

"We've been listening to reports about the assassinations, and to tell you the truth, I don't buy that lone-alien theory at all. What's your side of it?"

Nick told him, briefly.

"And you want the signal tracer to see if you've been bugged?"

Nick nodded.

"I've got a better idea," Joe said. "Take *Cynthia*."

"Your airplane?"

"Sure. Now that she's perfected I don't have any use for her. The process *toward* perfection, that's the important part. Become one with the machine; improve the machine, improve the self. Every machine is a step along the path."

"Your coming here today," Wanda continued, picking up

where he'd left off, "it's a sign. It's God's way of telling Joe to give up the airplane and move on to a new machine. If you get too attached to one machine, it stops your spiritual growth."

"We've always got to move on," Joe said, "until we reach the final machine, the Cosmic Mill."

"The Cosmic Mill?"

"This," he said, taking in everything with a wave of his hand. "I mean, once you've gotten into the Cosmic Mill, well, what else is there?"

"What indeed?" Nick agreed, totally mystified.

"Take it," Joe said, pressing the keys into Nick's hands.

"Take it," Wanda said, smiling warmly.

"I don't mean to seem ungrateful, but I think it's too slow. They'll catch up with me."

"No they won't. See, they'll be scanning the skies for MHD, which means they'll be looking for high-gauss magnetic fields and shit-kicker voltages. *Cynthia*'s biggest magnet is half a gauss, and her electrical system is twelve volts. That won't even tickle their instruments."

"Don't you see," Wanda said, "it's perfect! It's God's way of helping us both out, you with your escape, Joe with his spiritual development."

"You just want to reach the islands, right?" Joe was referring to a unique geological feature of Sifra Messa, a chain of islands which circled the planet at an altitude of ten thousand feet. They were an obvious place to hide since they were deserted, thousands in number and constantly in motion. "If you leave now, you'll reach them in a half hour. Cynthia will get you there fine as long as you're careful about landing."

Nick looked pensive; then he laughed.

"Why not? Things can't get more screwed up than they are now."

PART V
Escape to the Islands

❖ 1 ❖

The flying islands appeared overhead like quick low clouds, suddenly thickened into earth. They trailed streamers of roots and vines, and showered pebbles and clods of dirt. Nick pulled back on the steering wheel, nosing the plane into a steep climb in their direction. He glanced over his shoulder at Hali and Althea. None of them had ever ridden in a plane before, much less seen one, and they did not look happy: Hali sat with her eyes closed and every muscle of her face strained, as though her concentration alone were keeping them aloft; Althea observed their progress with wide-eyed terror and every bit of "chop" elicited from her as much of a scream as the ball gag would permit.

Nick, however, was enjoying himself. He had visited the islands countless times before—the same conditions that made it the perfect hiding place for fugitives made it the ideal retreat for lovers—but usually in MHD saucers, so smooth and silent and fast that one might as well have been riding an elevator. On the other hand, this great, rickety wooden bird, with its guy wires spread like harp strings and its taut silk skin, made him feel as though he were actually *flying*. Airplanes were risky.

Climbing to the islands, for example, he sensed that the plane was about to stall. He had stalled before, nearly smashing them all into the side of a mountain, so he knew what to do. He pushed up the throttle and lessened the angle of inclination until once again the climb was stable. The shadows of the islands passed over them like a giant raven's wing.

Suddenly the plane shot forward; they had been caught in the Island Stream, the hot wind that accompanied the islands in their circumferential flight. Nick backed off the throttle until they were flying at the same speed and the huge slabs of earth appeared to be standing still overhead.

Here the islands were closer together; their edges nearly interlocked, like pieces of broken pottery. The spaces between them were sometimes as narrow as ten feet, seldom as wide as fifty, and Nick would have to pass between them in order to rise above them. The task was made more difficult by the islands' tendency to shift slightly in relation to each other, occasionally closing up the spaces altogether, like ice floes. Even skilled pilots had been crushed between islands; in this unfamiliar, eccentric craft disaster seemed inevitable. Nick damned himself for ever giving up the MHD saucer.

He had chosen the largest piece of blue sky he could find, at the intersection of three islands. Now that he was scarcely twenty feet below it, the islands had begun to come together, the rough walls of earth closing in on them like a gargantuan vise. To change course would have meant hopelessly entangling the plane in the long dense growth of roots which trailed from the undersides of the islands. He had no choice but to continue climbing and try to get through the space before it closed, like a last-minute dash through the subway doors.

He jammed the throttle all the way forward. The engine coughed from receiving so much hydrogen so suddenly; for one heartrending second it almost died, then it picked up again with a screaming whine, and inch by inch, they rose.

Nick aimed as carefully as he could—the space between the islands couldn't have been more than the wingspan with inches to spare—and he was almost through when something tugged to the left; the wingtip had caught on the island. Nick felt himself losing control, he felt the plane beginning to cartwheel. He applied full right rudder and aileron to compensate and for an eternal instant the plane seemed to be standing on its tail. He tried to climb, but they had lost too much speed.

They were just emerging from the black shadows into the sun, into the clear sky above the islands. The slabs of earth were moving slightly faster, and if he could stay in the air another few seconds a fair-sized island would be beneath them. Five seconds would do it, but the engine was sputtering . . . four . . . three . . . two . . .

Nick killed the engine and the plane fell like a stone, ten feet to the surface of the island, and crashed there with a bone-shaking thunk.

He sat perfectly still, uttering small prayers.

Hali's voice came meekly from behind, "Is it over?"

"Yup."

She sighed deeply. "Life has not been without its small surprises since meeting you, Mr. Harmon."

"I try to keep it interesting," Nick said. "Shall we get out?"
He flipped open the canopy and the hot wind of the Island
Stream ruffled his thick black hair. He unhooked his safety
belt and stood up and Hali screamed. Like a see-saw perched
at the edge of a cliff, the airplane teetered horribly to the left.
Nick could see the surface of Sifra Messa rushing by ten
thousand feet below. He sat back down and the airplane
tilted back to the right.

"Don't move a finger," he whispered.

Then, keeping his weight as far right as possible, he shimmied out of the cockpit and lowered himself down the side of
the fuselage, holding the edge of the cockpit with his finger-
tips.

He saw the problem when he reached the ground. While
the right tire and the tail wheel sat firmly on earth, the
left tire hung over the abyss between islands. He ran to the
end of the right wing and leaned on it, and shouted for Hali
to help Althea out of the plane.

Empty, the plane was quite light. He and Hali, who had
paled almost to the color of a robin's egg, had little difficulty
rolling both wheels onto solid ground. They moved it under a
grove of palm trees and covered what still lay exposed with
fronds and enormous ferns. Then they collapsed.

Nick was exhausted, yet his blood was pounding so hard
he could see it against his closed eyelids, like a pulsing red
light. He felt Hali's hand take his own, her four fingers lacing
with his, and heard her whisper, "You are my hero, yes? My
knight with shining arms?"

"Yeah," Nick said, and laughed.

He felt her satin beak rubbing against his face, nipping at
his skin with the tip, and the excitement of fleeing turned easily into excitement of another kind. The sparkling effulgence
of her skin grew thicker; it was like a fine oil to the touch
and smelled like no perfume Nick could remember. And suddenly he understood the purpose of it: it was a kind of elec-
trolyte helping a strange sort of current pass between them
wherever their bodies touched.

When he was aroused beyond what he could bear, she
guided him into the silky wet fold between her legs. His organ fit strangely there, like a foot in the wrong shoe, yet in
the misfit there was additional pleasure. As the pressure of
the semen gathered in his groin, she placed her palms flush to

his temples, the effulgence sealing them in place, assuring complete contact, superconductivity, and he felt a warmth radiating from them, a sweet, ticklish electricity; and as it grew in intensity he began to understand why people died and the stars expanded and why the universe was divided into a male and female principle. She whispered to him in a strange sibilant language and when at last they came, perhaps a million years later, she bit a small piece out of his cheek.

II

Bound and gagged, Althea watched them make love. Later she tried to get his attention.

"Uhh! Uhh! Awahh eee!"

"Okay, okay," Nick said, rubbing his eyes.

Gingerly he plucked the ball gag out of her mouth. It was like uncorking a carbonated beverage or pulling a knothole out of a dam. She spat at him, she called him every horrible name she could think of, she even tried to bite him, but he pulled away too quickly.

"You shitty, fucking liar!" she screamed. "You promised to show me how the alien made love!"

"You just saw it," he said, smiling slightly.

"Untie me," she ordered. "I've got to pee."

Nick rolled her over on her stomach and set the combination lock so the cuffs sprang open. While he was kneeling down to untie her ankles she almost succeeded in opening his skull with a sharp rock, but she wasn't quite fast enough. Nick knocked her down and they grappled in the grass. She bit him and scratched him, but somehow he managed to get the cuffs back on.

"You'll have to pee like that," he said. "Sorry."

She tried a few kicks and when it became obvious that she was helpless, she screamed, "*Nicky Harmon, you are the most despicable, miserable and loathsome individual in the entire galaxy!*" and hobbled away.

❖ III ❖

Their island was roughly kidney-shaped and no more than a mile and a half in length. Of its two shallow ponds, one was nearly deep enough for bathing. The ground was covered with soft moss, and the air was filled with the indistinct voices of whisper ferns. The Brinko palms were half the height of their counterparts on the planetary surface, for the thinness of the air at that altitude was stunting to floral growth, dizzying to human minds. The luscious purple fruits of the palm were still out of reach, but by leaning all his weight on the rubbery trunk, Nick could lower them right into Hali's hands.

That night they gorged themselves until the purple sap ran down their chins, and they laughed and spat pits at each other, and served each other rainwater in the hollowed shells. There was a new freedom to their relationship, now that they had swept away the artifices of society. They were open and ingenuous, like puppies at play. And when, that evening, Nick called her "Ms. Hasannah," she cried, "For the love of God, call me *darling* or *space blossom* or *snookum nookums*, but please, *please*, no more Ms. Hasannah!"

And Nick laughed and promised to refrain.

He tried to feed the fruit to Althea, but she refused to eat. She wouldn't speak to Nick or even look him in the eye. He gave up in frustration and tied her to a palm so that he could sleep peacefully without worrying about her trying the rock trick again.

Then he and Hali made a bed on the moss, him sheltering her from the night with his broad body, feeling her warmth and smelling her smell, which was unlike any smell on the planet, yet somehow familiar, as though he had known it many many years ago. Both moons were visible, Schleiden white and still as an ancient civilization, Schwann racing madly across the heavens like a young culture, drunk with its own power. Stars winked through the fronds while whisper ferns made their secrets almost intelligible.

Althea's crying woke him an hour later. Listening to her

there in the dark, Nick came to his senses: he recalled that
she was more than a tool for achieving his own ends, she was
a thinking, feeling being. The fear and uncertainty to which
he had subjected her, through no fault of her own, appalled
him.

He disentangled himself from Hali's limbs and crept across
the moss to where he had tied her. A twig cracked under his
foot and she cried, "Who's there?"

"It's okay, it's only me. What's wrong?"

"Nothing." Silent, suddenly. She wasn't going to show any
weakness.

"Come on, Althea, tell me. I'm sorry about this. Look, I'll
probably get snuffed before the week is out and you'll have
your vengeance soon enough. In the meantime we might as
well—"

"Don't want vengeance," she whispered. "Don't want you
snuffed."

"Well, what do you want? Brinko fruit? Some water?"

"No."

"If I untie you do you promise not to try to kill me again?"
She sniffled a reply.

Nick undid all the bonds. Althea stretched, then curled in
a fetal position and cried and cried. Her hair was filled with
twigs and leaves, and her underwear was torn. Nick took off
his cape and covered her with it. Still she cried.

"I said I was sorry. Won't you tell me what it is?"

She murmured something.

Nick bent closer. "What?"

"My Raslow . . ."

"What's *Raslow*?"

"It's a skin preparation. . . . If I don't use it every night I
break out . . . I get pimples and blackheads and I look
horrid. . . ."

Nick tried not to laugh. What he had anticipated as a problem of human dignity had turned out to be only skin deep.
Still, it was obviously important to Althea, and who was he to
sit in judgment of another's priorities?

"Hali has something in her shoulder bag she uses on her
face. We could find out if . . ."

Althea stopped crying.

"How dare you suggest I use alien cosmetics! I'd sooner
rub dirt on my face. All my skin would probably peel off and

then she'd be happy, 'cause you'd get sick just looking at me
and she'd have you all to herself. . . ."
Tears returned, burning trails down her cheeks.
"So that's it," Nick said.
"What's it?"
"You're jealous."
"Of an alien? Never!"
Nick stroked her hair. "Don't cry."
"Not jealous," she mumbled.
"You must be so tired. Try to sleep."
He kissed her on the top of the head and crept away.

✿ IV ✿

"You people understand psi powers," Nick said next morning. "How would you go about opening a transdimensional
window? I don't know if the replicon Scolpes gave me has
taken effect, but I might as well start trying."
He was resting his head in Hali's lap while she fed him
slices of Brinko fruit. Cradled on her soft thighs, with a
warm breeze against his face and a palm rustling overhead, it
was difficult to worry about the fate of worlds; but to Nick's
credit, he forced himself.
"Ah," she said, kissing the juice off his lips, "the mysteri-
ous transdimensional window. The fact is, I know nothing except what I've seen at the Lifestyler Temples. Perhaps if you
can tell me more I can be of help."
"Fair enough," Nick said. He took a moment organizing
his thoughts. "Well, the early Lifestylers didn't have transdimensional windows. The TD gene wasn't invented until long
after Marvin Goldstein's death. You remember Marvin Goldstein?"
Hali nodded. "The Father of Lifestyling?"
"Right. But it was his partner, Lebachuck, who thought up
the TD gene. . . ."

During Goldstein's lifetime his primary interest was,
despite what the glorifying historians of Mutagen may have
written, turning a buck. His tastes—or what he assumed were

the tastes of the galaxy—had been shaped by his early experiences making porn films. He thought Lifestylers should be glamorous and well endowed, since that was the basis of Supplicant wish fulfillment. He believed that the concepts they embodied had to be extraordinarily simple, since the Supplicants were extraordinarily simpleminded. In other words he believed that, as a noted twentieth-century humorist once put it, "Nobody ever went broke underestimating the taste of the American public."

When Goldstein passed on, control of the company passed to Lebachuck, who, in a strange way, understood the public better than his predecessor. Instead of imagining what the public wanted, he acted upon what he himself wanted, assuming himself a fair representative of the public.

And what he wanted was not Lifestylers as superstars.

What he wanted was Lifestylers as gods!

He wanted them to be immortal, or at least incredibly long-lived, and he wanted them to have extraordinary powers. He wanted them to be worshippable. The way he saw it, as the galaxy grew increasingly technological, it left less and less room for magic. The human spirit was being strangled by its own tools. People needed to see a miracle now and then, they needed to know that existence was more than a narrow corridor between the cradle and the crypt, particularly now that the corridor was equipped with a slidewalk to hasten their passage.

Lebachuck was a man of curious contradictions: a brilliant scientist with an unyielding appetite for the truth—a skeptic concerning any new scientific theory until it had been proved experimentally and replicated countless times—yet also a Theosophist, a follower of the notorious Madame Blavatsky, the nineteenth-century Russian mystic who had spent much of her life in India learning the occult secrets of the fakirs and yogis. When asked to explain this wedding of opposites, he would say, "Science is a game, and to play a game well we must observe the rules. But if we step outside the game, we find a universe where anything is possible. The advent of anything, as we have learned from observing quantum particles, is limited only probablistically."

In his Theosophical studies, Lebachuck had come across a concept from Tibetan Buddhism, a middle ground between death and reincarnation called the Bardo, a land without time and place, haunted by hungry ghosts and guiding angels, beings of pure white light. Normally the Bardo was restricted to the newly dead, but by submitting themselves to regimes of austerity, celibacy, special diet and even physical torture, certain holy men or "shamans" managed to gain entrance to the Bardo during life.

Those who did enjoyed immortality, since in the land of the dead no man could die. The past and the future lay open to them, since this was a world without time. They were, in effect, godlike, and they were precisely what Lebachuck would have liked the Lifestylers to be.

After careful study of the austerities practiced by the shamans, Lebachuck came to the conclusion that subtle changes in the chemistry of the brain were brought about, particularly in the fluids which governed conductivity of the synapses. These changes, he reasoned, could be effected instantly, and with far less pain, through the creation of a "transdimensional" gene. RNA.

Naturally, between the gene's conception and its perfection came many many years of painstaking experimentation, of unsuccessful attempts ending in insanity and death for the subjects. And when at last success did come, the scientific community expressed doubts as to whether it was the Buddhist Bardo which had been reached; some believed it was a slight displacement of time, others that it was the antimatter universe which backed our own. Lebachuck himself said the distinction was semantic.

Years later, when Lebachuck was feeble and found his mind failing, he had himself injected with the transdimensional gene, opened a window in the air beside his wheelchair and rolled himself through it, never to be seen nor heard of again.

When Nick had finished his story, Hali was silent for some time, thinking. Finally she said, "We make things happen through *concentration*. It is a finite thing within the body, like blood or bile. It is a nimbus of energy which moves along the nervous system to wherever it is needed. When we eat, it moves to the stomach for digestion. When we think, it rises to the head. And when we make love"—she paused to smile languidly at Nick—"it goes to our sex. But usually," she continued, "usually concentration is diffused throughout the body. To gather it for a special task, we must make the body—and the mind—motionless. *One-pointed*. Sit like this."

Nick followed her example, assuming a crosslegged position on the soft moss, folding his hands in his lap as though he were holding an egg.

"Close the eyes, make the breath slow and even, turn the mind inward. Gather the concentration and move it through the body, along the limbs, up the spine, around the skull, until you find something—something which wasn't there before."

Nick opened his eyes. "Can't you be more specific?"

"Nicholas, darling, if I could I would flow inside you myself and search for it, but there are limits, yes? An Alta-Ty who had never associated with humans might have the power to do that; I do not."

All morning Nick sat in the striped shade of a palm and searched inside himself. He was surprised to find that by remaining physically motionless and cultivating a stillness of the mind, he became slightly euphoric. Perhaps he found the energy which was his *concentration*—he couldn't be sure; he certainly found nothing in the way of a transdimensional window. Perhaps the gene hadn't taken effect yet. When he stopped at noon his knees ached and his legs were filled with pins and needles. The inside of his mouth tasted like sandpaper. He decided to take a swim before returning to his inner exploration.

Pushing aside a screen of whisper ferns, he saw Althea kneeling by the side of the pool. He was about to call to her when he changed his mind and watched curiously. She was bending over a large, flat rock, grinding small piles of plants with a second stone which she moved with both hands, circularly.

There was whisper-fern blossom which she had ground into a red paste, a rich brown from the palm bark, purple from the Brinko fruit of course, and white powder from a brittle white crystal which grew on the north face of certain rocks.

She dipped her fingers in the white powder and, peering at her own reflection in the pond, carefully smeared it all over her face. She tried to leave an even coat, but the powder clung in certain places and fell away in others, leaving a

mottled surface. Next she dipped her index finger into the red
and wiped her lips with it, working the upper and lower lips
together as though she were sucking a lemon. The juice of
the Brinko fruit caked the powder around her eyes and the
brown bark simply refused to grind finer than peppercorns.
She took one last look at the grotesque mask she had made,
like some circus clown, or the decorated savage of a jungle
planet, and, frustrated beyond endurance, threw herself on
the ground and wept and wept. "Damn you, Nicky Harmon,"
she sobbed, "oh damn you, damn you."

He turned and crept away.

❖ V ❖

That afternoon he sat for hours, interrupting himself only to
stretch his legs when the pain of bent knees became unbearable. Around dusk he began feeling ill, a queasiness he attrib-
uted to sitting in one place all day; but as the night wore on,
the queasiness increased. The right side of his head ached and
his vision was overbright and flickery, as though someone
were shining a penlight in his eyes. These were, he realized
dismally, only the beginnings of the side effects Scolpes had
promised him. He had been hoping that perhaps he would be
excepted; no such luck.

Each day was worse than the previous. The throbbing in
his head grew so severe that he considered killing himself; the
brightness of his vision increased until he had difficulty
seeing; and something was happening to his throat which
made breathing an effort. When he sat in the manner Hali
had shown him and tried to turn his consciousness inward, all
he could perceive was discomfort. It was the pain of giving
birth and the pain of being born combined, for he was giving
birth to his new self. He imagined that he could feel his body
being renovated, DNA dividing, duplicating itself again and
again in a thousand million cells throughout the body.

Sleep was difficult and when it came, restless and uneasy.
Nick had a recurring dream of a stone dungeon with oak
door, iron hinges, oily black lock. Usually in these dreams he

had a keyring with a hundred keys and he had to try them one by one; other times, having no keys, he could merely pound on the door with his fists. He awoke unrefreshed, sunlight streaming like an ice pick into his brain.

After three days of this, a gleaming black police saucer sailed by some twenty miles east of them. Seeing it, Althea ran to the very edge of the island and began jumping up and down and screaming with all the voice she had. Her weight cracked the thin shelf of earth she was standing on and it gave way like a trap door. Fortunately the roots of the Brinko palms kept it hinged, and more of them, trailing above the ground, made convenient handholds for her to hang by until Nick could reach her and drag her back to solid ground.

The sight of the saucer must have rekindled thoughts of escape in Althea's mind; the following night Nick was awakened from one of his dungeon dreams (in this one he had a keyring, but the keys were all wormy and refused to stay still to be fit into the keyhole) by the sporadic firing of an internal-combustion engine. Hali rose first and started after the sound. She could run fast as an animal, even in the dark. Nick, trying to keep pace, stubbed his toes on roots and stones.

By the time they reached the moonlit clearing where they had left the airplane, that beautiful machine was lurching and bouncing toward the edge of the island. Althea must have sneaked the ignition key from Nick's pocket while he slept. Starting it had been no problem for her—the control array was similar to that of an MHD saucer—but flying it would be, particularly since there was not enough room for a take-off. She probably didn't understand that an airplane needed more space than an MHD craft; after all, the only airplane she had ever seen before was in the Technological Museum, side by side with a steamboat and a Model T Ford.

"Stop!" Nick screamed. "Althea, you'll kill yourself!"

The plane rolled on ahead of them on its big balloon tires, zigzagging to avoid the palms and a boulder like a big black knuckle, coming ever closer to the edge of the island and the ten-thousand-foot fall that waited there.

Perhaps Althea never really meant to escape; perhaps she had known all along that takeoff would have been impossible. The next moment a palm tree sliced halfway into the delicate wooden bonework of the wing, and the airplane, rotating on this pivot, ran head on into the largest palm on the island and came to an abrupt stop. The chattering of the engine ceased and the silence rang like the moment in a conversation when nobody can think of what to say.

Reaching the ship first, Hali climbed up the brackets and opened the hood of the cockpit. By the time Nick joined her she had her hands under Althea's arms and was lifting her out of the wreckage. She was unconscious. Her face was badly bloodied where it had smacked against the instrument panel.

They carried her a short distance to the pond, Nick reflecting on how many near-deaths in this accidentless future were actually cries for love. There they made a bed of moss and laid her down. He tore a square from his cape, his fine turquoise cape with the Lifestylers embroidered all over it, and, dipping it in the water, cleaned the caked blood from her face.

A ragged cut, startlingly red, began at the corner of her chin, transversed the perfect white flesh of her cheek and stopped just short of her eye. Her faultless nose was smashed at the cartilage and swollen like an egg, turning purplish green as they watched.

"Oh God," Nick whispered. "We don't even have a bandage."

"Yes," Hali agreed, "it will be difficult. I must have a few minutes alone."

And she walked away, leaving Nick kneeling by Althea's side.

"Wait a minute," he called after her. "Where are you going?"

But she didn't answer.

"Shit," he grumbled, "what a mess. How'd I ever get mixed up in this?"

"Nicky?" Althea was awake. "Nicky, my head hurts."

"Shh, don't worry, Althea. You'll be fine."

She raised herself on an elbow and groaned.

"Oh, I feel terrible. What happened? The airplane—I was going to take the airplane. But we're still on the island."

"You had an accident."

"An accident? But is the airplane all right?"

Nick hesitated.

"We'll never get out of here without the airplane. We'll die here. Nicky, do something."

"Relax. Everything's going to be okay."

He was reassuring himself as well as her. The cut across her face was bleeding lavishly and he was worried about infection. To be so far from medical machinery, so responsible for the situation, so helpless. He moistened the piece of cape and wiped her face with it.

"What's on my face?" she asked. She leaned over the pool, which was still as glass. Her reflection was brilliant in the moonlight, the huge scar, the swollen nose. She gasped. She reached for her face and touched the surfaces gingerly, wincing from the pain, trying to disprove the reality of it.

"No," she said, "no . . ."

"Just relax," Nick said.

He put his arm around her but she pulled away, crying, "*No!*"

Frantically she began to splash water on her face and wait impatiently for the ripples to subside so she could examine her reflection again, as though the wounds were stage makeup that might be washed away. She was so involved with this she did not notice Hali's return.

"Hold her down," Hali whispered to Nick.

Nick grabbed Althea by the shoulders and forced her onto her back. She screamed and kicked and scratched Nick's face with her nails. He sat on her, pinning her arms and legs as best he could. When Hali knelt by her head, she screamed, "Don't touch me, you filthy alien!"

Hali's four fingers grasped the crown of Althea's head like a vise. With the other hand she gathered the edges of the cut and held them in place for a few seconds, the time required, apparently, for the flesh to knit. She moved systematically along the length of the cut until it was entirely healed and all that remained was a long pink welt, no more serious than the mark left by sleeping on the fold of a sheet. After that she began to mold Althea's nose as though it were clay. Althea screamed. Her eyes rolled up and she bit into her lower lip. Then she fainted.

Having restored the nose to a semblance of its former shape, Hali rested her fingers on it and the swelling shrank, the discoloration faded. Then she climbed wearily to her feet.

"You know," Nick said, putting his arms around her, "you are the most truly generous person I have ever met in my life."

Hali smiled and rubbed her beak softly across his face.

Althea groaned. She shifted position, then opened her eyes and rose unsteadily to face them.

"You filthy, sadistic alien," she hissed, and slapped Hali across the face.

Nick snorted with disgust. He pushed her down to her knees and held her head a foot from the surface of the pool.

"Look at yourself," he ordered. "Hali did that—she healed you. You were mangled and she made you beautiful again. Even though you've been treating her like dirt for the past week."

Althea ran her fingers back and forth across the scar like a blind man reading braille. She faced Hali and tried to speak, but the words wouldn't come. She turned and ran.

Nick was grinning.

"I fail to see what is so amusing," Hali said, with a trace of annoyance.

"I'm sorry," Nick said, "but I can't help it. That headache I've had for the past week—it's gone."

The genetic change, he knew, was now complete.

❖ VI ❖

That night Nick dreamed of the dungeon. He stood in front of the oak door, without the keyring; yet for once he had no sense of impotency or frustration. He knew precisely what to do—almost as though he were receiving orders from an unknown being, orders direct to the subconscious.

"Open, door," he whispered, and with a wailing of hinges and rotting wood, the door swung wide.

What he saw then touched him like an icy hand: *Nothingness.*

His mind spun away from it like a top skimming the edge of a table, and he woke with a start. He lay awake in the dark, feeling the warmth of Hali's body and taking strength in it; come dawn, he knew, there would be no turning back. The window would open for him and he would have to enter that frightening void.

VII

"Keep an eye on Althea," Nick said, drawing the nerve gun from an inside pocket of his cape, "and if I don't come back . . ."

"If you don't come back," Hali said, "I will spend the rest of my life in misery, so please plan to return!" Thus she skirted the unpleasant thoughts in the back of both their minds.

"I love you," Nick said.

"And I, Nicholas—I would dare say, to hell with Alta-Tyberia! Let twenty million die so that the two of us can live out our lives together."

"Yeah, well, you may feel that way today, but I don't think you'd be so happy ten years from now."

Nick sat down crosslegged, but before he could begin concentration Hali knelt in front of him and kissed him.

"Please be careful."

"Nothing to it," he said casually.

"Shall I watch?"

"Might be better if you didn't."

Obediently Hali turned away. Nick wanted to call her back, but he saw that the longer he put it off, the more difficult it became.

No sooner had he closed his eyes than he felt that something was different within him. Power—that was it. His concentration gathered, like a light through a magnifying glass, into a white-hot point. Intuitively he knew what to do. He moved the point along his spine—it left a white-hot trail—and into his head. Then he moved it *out of his body,* into the air directly in front of him, level with his eyes. He opened his eyes—carefully, in order not to disturb his concentration—and was pleased to see it existing independently of him, a germinal window identical to the ones he had seen the Lifestylers create. As he broadened his concentration the point expanded into a disc the size of a saucer. It had the unmistakable flickering border, and within he could see the cold gray fog of the other side. He expanded the window further, until it was a foot in diameter, two feet, a yard. Then he rose to his feet and crept through it.

PART VI
Through the
Transdimensional Window

A chill penetrated like needles to his bone. He hugged himself for warmth, but it was no use; this chill was not of the body but of the soul. He was standing in the middle of a dense gray cloud and all around him, all he could see was gray. It had no depth to it; he could not tell where it began or where it ended or what, if anything, lay beyond it. He had heard that men maneuvering outside their ships in interstellar space, who had lost sight of their ships and later been recovered, had been driven insane by the endless, directionless void, and this possibility frightened him.

There was one sight, however, by which he could orient himself, and that was the window. It hung before him (though logically, having just passed through it, it should have been behind him) like a circular holovision screen filled with rich colors of sunlight and sky, swaying palms. Ever so cautiously he shrank the window to a pinpoint and opened it again, the way a mountain climber tests the rope by which swings his life. He dared not close it altogether.

He took a step toward it and the window receded. Scolpes had warned him of this peculiar effect, yet it still came as a shock. Right and left were reversed too; turning to the right, the window appeared to rush ahead of him; turning to the left, it returned twice as slowly to center.

Nick took another step toward the window and it moved farther away. He stepped away from it and it came closer. He giggled. Two more steps backward brought his head through the window so he was half in this world, half in the other. The hot wind of the Island Stream played across his face while the rest of his body suffered the awful chill. Then, the thought occurring to him that he might decapitate himself by accidentally closing the window in this position, he withdrew.

He walked toward the window until it was a bright coin of sunlight lying on the cotton grayness, and stopped. What to do next? He dared not turn his head for fear of losing view of the window, and the same reason stopped him from moving any farther away.

He had supposed, naively perhaps, that a Lifestyler would be waiting for him just this side of the window. After all, they saw the future; they would know Nick was on his way. He reminded himself that they were godlike, not gods; prescient but not omniscient. They couldn't be expected to keep track of the whereabouts of everybody on Sifra Messa—and why should Nick assume that his own dilemma was of more importance than anyone else's? Certainly we are the stars of our own lives, yet to turn the rest of the world into supporting players is to have delusions of grandeur.

If only he could find another point of orientation, then he would not be afraid of penetrating more deeply into this strange land. There had to be other landmarks, or else how could the Lifestylers navigate? He stared very hard at the grayness in front of him, trying to distinguish some irregularity in it. After a few moments he thought he saw a blur of color. Focusing on it, he gradually perceived that it was constituted of a rapid succession of images. Despite the speed with which they flashed by he found that his eyes could single out one image in particular and leisurely watch it unfold.

It was an image of people—no, they were robots; there was a stiffness, a mechanical regularity to their movements. The world they walked on had a black, airless sky and a surface swirled like volcanic glass. The landscape was flat as far as the eye could see, stripped of buildings and vegetation and people. The only motion was the motion of the robots marching at random back and forth and around in circles. Occasionally two or more stopped to converse, working their jaws, moving their hands in a parody of human conversation; yet Nick could hear no words.

All this came to him as a sort of waking dream, all totally vivid and real; at the same time he could feel the chill of the grayness and watch, from the corner of his eye, the distant, reassuring light of the transdimensional window.

Now the part of Nick's consciousness which was synchronized with the "robot world" plunged down through the glassy surface beneath their ponderous mechanical feet, down through the earth, down to the very bowels of the planet. There he found, locked away like jewels in a vault, row after row of life-preserver jars. Floating in each of them was a naked body, soft and fragile and white as a worm. They were men and women and children, although the characteristics of sex and age had been dulled beyond distinction by so many years of soaking. And they constituted the entire humanity of the planet. Machines tended their life-support systems, other machines tended the machines tending them, and so forth and so on, an almost infinitely redundant system of maintenance.

Nick found it within his power to enter the mind of one of the bottlemen. The next instant Nick found himself back on the surface, viewing the world from within the spherical metal head of a robot. Apparently the robot was the bottleman's *representative*, his eyes and ears, his arms and legs. The bottleman was living out his life through this steely surrogate.

Previously the machines had all looked alike, hardly human; now they appeared as people, vital and alive. Where before he had seen only a barren horizon, now, through the mind of the bottleman and the eyes of the robot, he beheld a city of pastel-tinted towers and lush green parks. Unassisted, men rose to the highest spires, weightless as soap bubbles; others rode across the land in seashell-shaped carriages drawn by serpents with shimmering skins. The bottleman must have created these lavish embellishments from his imagination, the way one doodles to fill a blank space of paper.

How, Nick wondered, could such a world have ever come into existence? He wished he could have spent more time investigating it, but he had loitered too long already. As he withdrew his consciousness, the world faded into a stream of images, the images into a blur of colors.

To his relief the transdimensional window still shone in the distance. Furthermore, the flow of colors, which was far more distinct now that his eyes had adjusted to the grayness, flowed nearby it. This might be the means of orientation he had been hoping for; he could follow it and later it would lead him back home, like the trail of bread crumbs in a fairy tale he had once heard.

He started along the colors, moving in the direction of the window, walking with an even pace and counting his steps to maintain some sense of time and distance. Due to direction reversal, the window soon vanished in the distance and Nick was forced to rely on the flow of colors alone. He prayed that it was a spatially stable phenomenon.

After three thousand steps Nick stopped to rest. For amusement he allowed himself to gaze into the flow, and once again his eyes fixed on an image, an image of people running. . . .

The planet was Terra, capitol of the UFW—he recognized

it from pictures. Sirens screamed *Bahweeeee! Bahweeeee!* and everywhere was chaos. People ran helter-skelter through the streets, convening on the giant central square in front of the senate building. There, metal doors, installed in anticipation of this moment, had opened to reveal the mouth of a well nearly a mile in diameter. Without hesitating millions hurled their children and loved ones into that black abyss and leapt in after them. For a few hundred feet they fell like stones; then some force broke their momentum and they drifted gently. Seconds later the doors clanged shut; those who had not reached the well in time, the aged, the infirm and the crippled, crawled on top of the doors and banged with hands and heels. But the doors were shut and sealed for all of time to come.

Meanwhile at the edge of the solar system a drone warship of alien origin, using powerful tractor beams, dragged a black hole into orbit. This was the ultimate weapon, this primordial black hole, no larger than a proton yet with a mass of a billion tons. It had been emitting antiparticles ever since the dawn of the universe; now, however, the process would be accelerated. The warship began to drain off antiparticles at a fabulous rate and the black hole evaporated almost instantly, exploding with an energy equivalent to ten million one-megaton hydrogen bombs, and flooding that entire sector of the galaxy with high-energy gamma rays.

As Nick watched, the surface of Terra—and of a thousand neighboring planets—was leveled. The shock wave did most of the damage, knocking moons out of orbit, blowing away buildings as though they were paper and uprooting whole forests of trees. Then came the heat, igniting what vegetation was left, cremating flesh, boiling the oceans and turning the earth to molten lava. Finally the whole planet glowed like a lump of steel in a furnace. Yet deep in the core of the world, mankind survived. . . .

Nick yanked his consciousness away. Each image in the flow told a story, and it was all too easy to become involved—the stories seemed so real.

He continued along the flow of colors, keeping an even pace and counting his steps. At five thousand steps he spied three figures far ahead, examining the flow. They looked like finely detailed dolls posed on a bed of gray cotton. He breathed more easily; they were Lifestylers.

When he was closer they waved to him with bittersweet

smiles. There was Squire Stolid, a forty-foot obelisk of flesh, legless, but with arms emerging from his smooth side walls and a kindly bas-relief face near his summit; and Lady Lovelorn, whose great saucer eyes could show you pictures of the one you loved; and Captain Cranium, his tiny body dwarfed by a supercephalic head, like a visitor from some distant future.

Lady Lovelorn greeted him with an outstretched hand.

"We've been waiting for you, Nicholas Harmon."

Her eyes were gray holes, little transdimensional windows in which images swam like silverfish. Her hair was long, silky, silver. She was nearly two feet taller than Nick—all the Lifestylers were larger than life—and emaciated; the skin cleaved beneath her cheekbones and her ribs became prominent whenever some gesture pulled the gossamer gown tight across her chest.

"How did you know?" Nick said. His own voice sounded tiny, flat. There were no surfaces anywhere to give it resonance.

"We knew from the instant you decided to use Althea Clinger as a hostage." As she spoke, Hali's face appeared deep within Lady Lovelorn's eyes. Nick felt a pang, missing her. "It made a new stochastic stream," she continued, "and a possibility of salvation for the galaxy." Lady Lovelorn smiled. "It was brave of you to come."

"Excuse me," Nick said, "but what's a stochastic stream?"

"This," she said, pointing to the flow of colors. "They tell the future—in *that* direction"—she pointed in the direction Nick had just come from—"and the past if you follow it the other way."

Nick looked puzzled.

"I think I'd better explain," Captain Cranium said. "Here on the other side, time has a physical parameter. These streams of color—stochastic streams, we call them—are actually sequences of events that will happen, or may happen. Usually several alternative futures are possible so there are several streams running parallel. Actually there are an infinite number of streams, but only the most probable ones are bright enough to be visible.

"Now, you must understand, even the visible streams are mutable. A casual decision by somebody in the real world may cancel the brightest stream out of existence, or create a whole new branching. That's what happened when you de-

cided to use Althea Clinger as a hostage. One particular
stream seemed so bright we didn't think anything could
change it, and the next instant a new stream had sprung into
view, just as bright."

"You mean I'm going to change history?" Nick asked.

"I mean you *may* change history."

"We *hope* you will change history," Squire Stolid rumbled,
from high above them.

"And what is this history I'm going to change?"

"It's the stream you followed to meet us," Captain
Cranium said.

"You mean that stuff I saw, the people in the life-preserver
jars and the robots wandering around?"

"Yes, that is the distant future of that particular stream."

"And not one I look forward to," Squire Stolid boomed.

"And the people jumping down the well?" Nick asked.
"The exploding black hole?"

"The same future, a more recent view. You see, you were
following the stream backward through time. The explosion
made Terra—and most of the other planets in this sector—
uninhabitable. The people who were hiding at the core im-
mortalized themselves in life-preserver jars and built robots to
be surrogates for them on the surface."

"Do you mean to tell me," Nick asked incredulously, "that
this is really a possible future?"

Captain Cranium nodded his huge skull.

For a time Nick was speechless. Finally he demanded,
"But how? How could it happen?"

"Look here," Captain Cranium said, pointing a delicate finger to a certain point in the stochastic stream.

Nick's eyes singled out an image. . . .

The giant central square in front of the senate building, yet
now the streets were packed with cheering crowds. Plasma
fireworks exploded high above the planet while battalions of
police marched back and forth in formation to the beat of an
electric Bucla band. The biggest hologram Nick had ever seen
hung from the facade of the senate building; the face on it
jutted its chin almost to the middle of the square. That
face—Nick recognized it, the crinkly eyes and the toothsome
smile. He wasn't surprised that Johnny Quog had been elect-
ed president of the Federation; what did surprise him was the
size of the inaugural celebration. *If* it was an inaugural
celebration. . . .

A young man stepped out on the balcony of the senate building and the crowd fell silent. "I now present to you," he said in solemn tones, "Johnny Quog, Imperial Emperor of the Universe!"

The cheer was deafening.

"Imperial Emperor of the Universe?" Nick said. "Is that a joke?"

Captain Cranium shook his head. "I'm afraid not. He seized total power two months after the election. This is his official 'coronation.' The man is a paranoid schizophrenic. Listen to what comes next."

Nick returned his attention to the sequence. Johnny Quog was standing on the balcony, smiling his famous smile. He acknowledged the crowd with outstretched arms.

"The glorious human race," he began, "has spread its seed throughout the Milky Way and we have even visited the Greater Magellanic Cloud! We have achieved what no other planetary civilization has approached—freedom from our birthplace world. And why were we given the ingenuity, the resources and the ambition to perform this miraculous feat? Because we were destined, I say we were *destined* to rule the universe and bring Terran civilization to all the savage and downtrodden creatures of the cosmos! We must unite the galaxy! We must bring all sentient beings under a common rule—only then can there be lasting peace."

Lasting peace—the words echoed off the face of the senate building.

"That lasting peace," Captain Cranium said, "never came to be. Certain 'savage and downtrodden creatures' were less than eager to be put under Terran rule. They decided to fight for their freedom, a war that nearly annihilated mankind and half a dozen other races."

"You said the future could be changed," Nick exclaimed, drawing away from the stream. "You can warn the people about Johnny Quog. You're Lifestylers—they'll listen to you."

"We tried," Captain Cranium said wearily. "Lex Largesse tried. Sir Etherium tried."

Then it was all clear to Nick. "So that's what Lex wanted to tell Scolpes. And that's why he was assassinated. But you're still going to tell the galaxy, aren't you?"

Nick looked from face to face. The Lifestylers avoided his gaze.

"We can't," Captain Cranium said finally. We'd be killed

off one by one."

"But billions of lives are at stake!"

"Try to understand," Lady Lovelorn said, placing her hand on his arm. "We are nearly immortal. If one of *you* is killed you lose twenty or thirty years of life. If I am killed I lose *several thousand*. Try to see how precious life is to us!"

"Furthermore," Squire Stolid rumbled, from high above Nick's head, "we don't like to involve ourselves in politics. We're artists. Oh, it's been tried in the past. There have been political Lifestylers, but they've always been critical failures. Too polemical. Preachy, if you know what I mean."

"We're on your side," Lady Lovelorn reassured Nick. "We'll do everything we can to help you change the future. But suppose you don't succeed? Quog becomes dictator. Billions are killed. After it's all over you'll be dead, but we'll only be a couple of hundred years older. Why, I don't even suppose I'll be getting wrinkles. I'll be able to make a comeback. I mean, no matter what happens to civilization and politics, they'll always need Lifestylers."

Reflected in her eyes now, Nick noticed, was an image of herself.

He couldn't believe his ears. These people whom he had worshipped all his life were self-absorbed, infantile egotists. Fortunately for them the public never glimpsed them backstage.

"I hope you don't think," Nick said, "that I'm going to run back to the real world and tell them what I saw—because first off, they'd laugh at me; then they'd shoot me. You're the only ones who can do it, and I get the feeling you're all digging in for a thousand-year nap."

"Don't make us out to be villains," Captain Cranium said. "We're afraid for our lives. You'd be too if you were in our place."

Nick decided he wouldn't, but remained silent.

"Tell you what we will do, though," Cranium continued. "If you find the man who murdered Lex and Sir Etherium and show us that he's safely confined, then we'll come out and alert the people."

"Well, that's just great," Nick said. "The election is next week. You expect me to find the murderer and put him away in eight days when I can't even show my face anywhere?"

"You're our only hope, Nicholas Harmon," Lady Lovelorn said.

"Well then, I guess that's that." Nick shrugged his shoulders, turned and started back along the flow of colors which led to the transdimensional window.

❖ II ❖

It was about noon when Nick emerged from the window, judging by the position of the sun. He had no sooner shrunk the window out of existence when he heard behind him a hissing sound. Hali raised her head from a clump of whisper ferns and beckoned to him.

"What are you doing down—" Nick said.

But before he could finish she had grabbed him by the hand and dragged him behind the ferns. Althea was kneeling beside her; they both looked worried.

"What's going on?" Nick said.

"Visitors," she whispered, pointing to a clearing to the left of them.

A swankily appointed MHD camper was parked only a hundred feet from where they crouched. A hammock had been rigged between the landing-ramp rail and a Brinko tree which bent almost double under the weight, and basking in the hammock, an iced drink in one tentacle, a best-selling microfiche in another and a dainty sandwich in the third—watercress on white bread with crusts removed—was a Roolik.

All Rooliks looked the same to Nick, the round hairless head with bulging eyes, the skin of diamond-shaped scales which grew more and more wrinkled as it approached the year molting. Two tentacles on the left, one on the right. The third tentacle was for picking your pocket, as the old joke went, while you were being embraced with the other two. This particular Roolik wore tanning-tights with cutouts, a gaudy jeweled codpiece and the most ostentatious cape Nick had ever seen.

The Roolik's wife stood beside the hammock dabbing moistener on his scales with an applicator bottle. Physically she was identical to him, only a head shorter. She wore a Terran-style sundress with three puffy sleeves. Their two children, diminutive versions of themselves, sat nearby, playing contentedly with toy spaceships. The presence of additional Rooliks was implied by a holovision blaring from inside the camper, probably a grandparent or two. As a rule, Rooliks had large families and liked to take them all on vacations—to act as unpaid servants for the master of the household.

"What a happy little family," Nick whispered. "I wonder how they'd feel about lending us their camper?"

"That's what we were thinking," Althea said conspiratorially.

It appeared that mutual need had smoothed relations between the two women.

"Where's the gun?" Nick whispered.

Hali slipped it into his hand and tapped him on the cheek with her bill for luck.

Crouching, he crawled toward the clearing. They didn't notice until he was almost on top of them; then the female Roolik shrieked and tossed the bottle into the air.

Nick stood up. "Line up over there," he said, flourishing the nerve gun. "Do as I say and you won't get hurt."

The male Roolik rose warily from the hammock and put a protective tentacle around his wife. The children ran behind him, hugging his legs with fright. Nick hoped they wouldn't test him; he knew he couldn't fire the gun at them, even if it meant his own life.

"What do you want fwom us?" the Roolik asked.

The children were crying with fear, odd little snorting sounds.

"Just stay put and keep quiet."

Nick glanced at the entrance to the saucer.

"My gwandmother's the only one inside," the Roolik said. "She's just an old lady."

"Tell her to come out."

"Come on out, Gwandma," the Roolik shouted helpfully.

The next instant something came rolling down the ramp so fast Nick didn't have time to react; it knocked him on his back and sent the gun flying to the feet of Father Roolik, who snatched it up in a tentacle. The next instant Hali and Althea were kneeling by Nick's side, rubbing his hands and patting his cheeks, asking him if he had been hurt?

"Ohhhhhh," Nick said, and, "What happened?"

The answer was a life-preserver jar containing a wizened Roolik grandmother, curled up like a dried lizard. The stereoptic camera on top of the jar was aimed at Nick and the speaker below it was emitting an emotionless rasping—they had not yet learned to pass feelings through wire—which Nick took to be a cackle.

"Heh-heh-heh, serves you wight, humie, twying to twick a Woolik . . ."

"Shut up, you old hag," Althea snapped. "Can't you see he's been hurt?"

Nick stumbled to his feet, groaning and rubbing his hip.

"Now it's your turn to line up," Father Roolik said. He inspected them one by one at gunpoint. When he reached Hali his little hole of a mouth made gulping motions, a sign of excitement in Rooliks.

"My, my, my, what have we here? A wavishing alien cweature. What planet do you call home, my dear?"

"That, sir," Hali replied, "is none of your damn business."

The Roolik stepped back and considered her, rubbing his chin with a free tentacle.

"I've seen your face," he said thoughtfully. "But of course! You're the Alta-Tybewian. You're the one who helped her escape, the senator's son. And you must be the police chief's daughter. I've seen tapes of you on the holovision. You must have wanted my camper for your getaway—am I wight?"

"Brilliant," Nick said.

"Isn't this exciting?" the Roolik said to his wife. "We're involved with despewate cwiminals! Get the camewa."

Obediently she disappeared into the saucer and returned a few seconds later with a split-beam holosnapper. Father Roolik made a series of what Nick imagined were considered ferocious faces while Mother Roolik snapped picture after picture. Then Father Roolik posed the children with carefully coached looks of terror.

"What about me?" Grandma cackled. "I'm the one who knocked him down, why don't I get in any of the pictures?"

"How many times do I have to explain to you?" Father Roolik said, exasperated. "You're dead and dead people don't photograph well."

But she kept complaining and finally Father Roolik allowed Mother Roolik to snap Grandma posing with the three captives.

"Look," Nick said wearily, when Mother Roolik started on her second role of film, "why don't you just give us to the police and get it over with? The press will take plenty of pictures of you."

"Because," the Roolik said, "I'm not so sure that's what I

want to do. How'd you like to make a deal?"

How'd you like to make a deal? Impossible to talk to a Roolik for more than five minutes without that phrase coming up.

"We don't have any money," Nick said.

"I don't want money," the Roolik said. He snaked a tentacle in Hali's direction. "I want her."

"Out of the question," Nick said.

"Why don't you let the lady make up her own mind? One night together—and in the morning I'll take you anywhere you want to go. Furthermowe, I pwomise not to say a word to the authowities." The Roolik turned to Hali and continued, "Ever make it with a Woolik? We can be a lot of fun. Of course I'll want my wife to holotape the whole expewience. It might be vewy educational for the kids too."

"I'll break your fucking neck," Nick said.

Hali restrained him. "Nicholas, simply because we are lovers, this does not mean you own me. It is *my* body and *my* property to do with as I see fit. I believe this would be a very small sacrifice for a very great reward."

"She's a wise one," the Roolik said.

"I won't let you do it," Nick said.

"It's *my* decision," Hali insisted, "and I've decided that . . ."

"Yes?"

"That I must think it over."

"You may have until midnight," Father Roolik said. "Wap on the saucer door and give me your decision. In the meantime you may do as you like. I'll take care of this." *This* was the nerve gun, which he stuck into the elastic waistband of his tights.

The Roolik family climbed into the saucer, father bringing up the rear. "I'll be counting the hours till midnight," he called, before closing the hatch.

"Fucking Rooliks," Nick muttered. He kicked a stone with his toe. "He's not going to lay a tentacle on you."

"Nicholas! It is *my* decision."

Discussion was suspended while they gathered Brinko fruit and empty shells filled with rainwater. Then they sat under the palm tree which was "home" for them on the island, to eat and to listen to Nick's description of his adventures behind the transdimensional window. As he talked, Nick couldn't help but wonder at the change which had come over Althea since her failed escape. No longer was she the vain, conceited little girl who could not pass a mirror without lingering to regard herself from every different angle, who would not raise a finger to help another without some tangible, immediate reward in the offing.

When he came to the part of the story about Johnny Quog declaring himself emperor, Althea was deeply upset; her father, Chief Clinger, was one of Quog's staunchest supporters. Most teenage girls would sooner die than admit their fathers to be capable of wrongdoing. Nick made it easier by suggesting that Chief Clinger probably had no idea what Quog was planning; perhaps Quog himself had not yet thought of it. After all, they were dealing with a future which did not yet exist.

At twenty-three hours by Nick's wristwatch, Althea yawned and excused herself. She had been sleeping beneath a second palm grove, near enough to scream for help if need be, far enough away to assure Nick and Hali their privacy.

Now that they were alone, and with only one hour until midnight, Nick began to argue. He pleaded with her not to meet the Roolik, then he forbade it. He said that if she wanted to go then she couldn't really love him; silly, since obviously the opposite was the case. Finally at a loss for words, he put his arms around her and held her tight. For some time she struggled to get loose, banging his chest with her fists— rather gently it seemed—but then her blows turned to caresses.

After they had finished making love she asked, "Why is it that humans, who have nothing but contempt for every other alien species, bear such respect for the Rooliks? I find Rooliks to be mercenary, exploitive, materialistic and cruel."

"We recognize in Rooliks," Nick replied, "ourselves."

❖ III ❖

Nick had been sitting outside the saucer for some time next morning before the landing ramp whirred softly to the ground. A moment later the Roolik appeared wearing a bathrobe, holding the nerve gun in one tentacle, a cup of stimu-caff in another and the best-selling microfiche (a scandalous novel about a Lifestyler with an insatiable appetite for young female Supplicants) in the third.

Nick met him at the foot of the ramp.

"Did you sleep well?" the Roolik said.

"Cut the crap and let's get going. We're ready."

"What's the huwwy? Have some bweakfast with us. After a night like last I need my pwotein."

"What are you talking about?"

"It was one of the finest nights of lovemaking I've ever ex-pewienced." He looked dreamily off into space. "I can't wait to watch the films of it."

"What?" Nick said. He had been up nearly all night with Hali. Was it possible that at some point he had drifted off to sleep, that she had stolen from his side in the moonlight and gone to the Roolik's bed? He tried to remember.

"Good morning, Nicky."

Althea was standing at the top of the ramp, wearing a matching bathrobe. Her hair was clean and lustrous; apparently she had showered.

"Ah, my little love nut," the Roolik said, turning to face her. "You awe a late sleeper."

The tentacle holding the stimu-caff put down its cup. The tip of it snaked once around her waist and probed the opening of her bathrobe.

"Stop it!" she shrieked, yanking the squirming thing away. Hurriedly she regained her composure and, shaping her mouth into a loving smile, murmured, "You tired me out, darling."

Nick noticed the rings under her eyes.

"When she came to the saucer," the Roolik continued, "in place of the Alta-Tybewian, I was dweadfully disappointed. I wanted to send her away and forget the whole thing, but she was persuasive. Now I'm glad I didn't—awen't you, my little love nut?"

"I sure am," Althea said. "You're the most terrific lover I've ever had."

"Particulawly flattewing," the Roolik added, "when you consider that our species is normally egglaying."

"I never would have known it," Althea said, "if you hadn't told me."

"As far as I'm concerned," the Roolik said to Nick, "you've held up your part of the bargain. I'll take you whew-ever you're going. And on my honor, I won't bweathe a word to the authowities."

"Mlrpa, darling," Althea said, "do you mind if I go for a

little stroll with Nicky before we sit down for breakfast? I'd like to tell him about all the fabulous things you did while they're still fresh in my memory."

"Of couwse, my little love nut. Huwwy back."

He suavely blew her a kiss on the tip of his free tentacle and climbed back into the saucer.

"What's the rush?" Nick called. Althea was walking away from the saucer so quickly he almost had to run to keep up with her. When a rise of earth had hidden them from view, Althea fell to her knees and vomited her guts out. Nick held her head and stroked her hair, murmuring that she had indeed done a beautiful thing.

❖ IV ❖

By noon Hali, Althea and Nick, as well as the entire family of Rooliks, were safely inside the observation bubble of the saucer, watching the island receding in the distance, losing itself among thousands of other, identical islands.

"That was our honeymoon suite," Hali whispered in Nick's ear. "I will always remember it."

Father Roolik operated the control console with two tentacles while the third wandered mischievously into the openings of Althea's dress. The garment had been donated by Mother Roolik to cover Althea's shredded underwear; it was gray and fit too tight across the bosom, too loose at the belly and too short at the knees. Althea retained her smile and backed politely away, but the tentacle followed her to the very perimeter of the room.

The children sat with their faces squashed against the glass for a better view, Mother Roolik beside them, holding and stroking them with her various arms. The blare of the holovision from below revealed Grandma's position. None of the family seemed too concerned by Father's persistent lechery.

Later that day Nick, finding himself alone with Father Roolik in the observation bubble, took the opportunity to ask a question he had been puzzling over since the day before.

"Yesterday, when your mother nearly ran me down with her life-preserver jar—how did she know I was standing there?"

"She has vewy stwong psi powers. Why, if I make a dispawaging wemark about her she knows it, even if she's fifty miles away. And," he added ruefully, "she doesn't let me forget it, either."

Nick nodded sympathetically. "Sounds tough. I'm surprised, though: I never knew you people had psi powers."

"We don't. Only Gwandma has it, and only since she's been in the life-pweserver jar. I've thought about it a lot but I don't know why it is."

"*Concentration,*" Nick murmured.

"Pardon me?"

"No bodily functions to diffuse the concentration. No breathing or digesting food or making love. So it's all available for the mind."

"I'm afwaid I don't follow."

But Nick's thoughts were outpacing his ability to explain. Piece after piece tumbled into place, and suddenly he knew who had murdered the Lifestylers, knew it beyond the faintest doubt.

"Will you give me back the nerve gun?" he asked with excitement.

After considerable hesitation and repeated assurances that it would not be used against himself or his family, the Roolik agreed.

"And I'd like you to keep Hali and Althea with you for the next couple of days. I'll be in danger and I want to know that they're safe."

"How could I wefuse? Both women, simultaneously—what an expewience!"

"Now wait a minute, I didn't mean *that.*"

"If they cwave me, you don't expect me to stop them?"

"Yeah, and if they don't crave you, I don't expect you to force them."

"Sir!" he harumphed, "I am a Woolik!" Then, in a confidential tone, "I expect the human woman has told the Alta-Tyberian about my wemakable sexual techniques. She won't be able to wesist twying it for herself. But I would never fowce anyone."

"Another thing," Nick said. "We've got to change our destination."

The Roolik was surprised when Nick told him where he wanted to go; nevertheless he kept his word and began plotting a new course on the charts.

PART VII
The Sleeping Assassin

It was midnight when the saucer swooped low over the rambling ivory castle. It hovered ten feet above the lawn while Nick leaped from the hatch; then it rocketed skyward again. On catlike feet he crossed the lawn and came to an arch which sloped to a second-story window. The arch was decorative, but in his childhood it had facilitated many nighttime escapades; tonight it would do so again. It took him only minutes to shimmy to the top. He slipped in through the window and crept down the hall, the nerve gun a reassuring weight in his waistband.

He pressed the door slide outside his father's study and entered silently. The room was dark except for one light which drew a bright parabola on the senator's giant desk. The senator's life-preserver jar was parked behind the desk, the senator himself shriveled like a fetus within the milky fluid. Nick wondered if he was aware of his presence. There was no way of telling whether he was awake or asleep or if he slept at all for that matter. The camera eyes were aimed roughly in Nick's direction, but that didn't mean anything.

"Nicholas." The name crackled from speaker atop the jar, startling him. "How are you?"

"No complaints."

"I am pleased that you have decided to turn yourself in to the police. I was worried about you being hurt. Now at least I know you will be safe."

"Safe and lobotomized."

"The mind-wipe, I've been told, is painless. The loss of forty or fifty IQ points is a small price for a technique that has rid our society of crime. Afterward one experiences a marvelous sense of peace and well-being."

"Sounds great," Nick said.

For a time they gazed at each other across the massive desk. In addition to numerous holocubes for calls and information retrieval, the desk contained a laser projector which transmitted a life-sized image of the senator to the senate building on Terra, during the times when that house was in session.

On the wall behind the desk hung the official portrait of
the incumbent president, a nondescript little man with glasses
and a milquetoast expression, and a portrait of self-assured
Johnny Quog posing with the senator, and a portrait of the
senator before his death, a different man altogether, standing
with his arm around the waist of a beautiful woman. She was
tall, with thick black hair; the resemblance to Nick was obvious.

"I didn't come here to turn myself in," Nick said. "I've
found out who murdered the Lifestylers. It wasn't Hali."

"Oh? And what makes you think that?"

Nick felt perspiration break out all over his body. It was
impossibly difficult playing cat and mouse with this man in
the jar. He was dead! He had no emotions! Even if he had
wanted to smile or frown or give any clue to his thoughts, the
nerve paths were simply no longer there; the muscles no longer functioned. No wonder most of the politicians were drawn
from the ranks of the dead.

"The police decided that Hali did it," Nick summarized,
"because she was the only person on the planet with psi powers. Whoever killed the Lifestylers needed psi powers to work
the psychic field amp. Sure she was there when the Lifestylers
were murdered, but that doesn't mean anything. The psych
field amp works remotely; it'll even work in the future, that's
what Scolpes told me. And the business about her hating humans is ridiculous. She's one of the most compassionate
people I've ever met. So it boils down to the psi powers.

"But suppose there was somebody else who could work the
psych field amp, somebody who had a *real* motive for mur-
dering Sir Etherium and Lex Largesse? You see, the Lifestylers were reading the future one day and they learned some
very dangerous information about Johnny Quog's political
ambitions. Next, I imagine, they got in touch with certain
Peace Party officials and told them that unless Quog dropped
out of the elections, they would alert the rest of the galaxy.

"Quog didn't pay any attention to them, so the Lifestylers
went ahead—but before they could talk, two of them were
murdered and the rest scared enough to keep their mouths
shut. The point is, the assassinations were *political*; the only
people who stood to gain were supporters of Johnny Quog."

Nick paused, hoping that Senator Harmon would prevent
him from continuing, but the speaker grill remained silent.

He took a deep breath. It was becoming more and more difficult to speak.

"All humans have psi powers, but usually their concentration is too diffuse to make use of it. That's because their
bodies are busy moving around and breathing and digesting
food. But this particular person's body was mechanically
maintained so his concentration had nothing to distract it.
Naturally he never let on that he had the power; it was too
useful a tool. And he was such a respectable old gentleman
nobody ever dreamed he was a murderer."

Nick could say no more.

Almost a minute later Senator Harmon crackled, "And
who is this person, Nicholas?"

Nick's voice was barely audible.

"You."

Another long silence elapsed before the senator spoke
again.

"I've always thought you were a fool, Nicholas. You didn't
survive your first term of medical school. Your only interests
seem to be rocket polo and women. Your job at Mutagen
was a result of my personal connections, and only my influence has stopped you from being fired. Yet you've unraveled
this incident quite nicely. The only element you've neglected
is your friend Ms. Hasannah. It was not by whim that we
chose her as our sacrificial lamb. We intend to demand reparations from the Alta-Tyberians, reparations for the loss of
our Lifestylers."

"Pallinite," Nick said.

"Indeed. We have a fleet of warships standing ready. As
soon as Ms. Hasannah is apprehended and tried, we will
dispatch them for her planet and the vast resources of pallinite will be ours."

"But it won't give you military superiority," Nick objected.
"I've seen the future myself—I've seen what will happen. The
surfaces of our planets will become uninhabitable. We'll all
be living underground in bottles while robots act out our
lives."

"Yes, Nicholas, but I am already living in a bottle. It won't
make any difference to me."

"I won't let you," Nick said, starting toward him. It would
be simple enough to pull out a few tubes and let the milky

fluorocarbons drain onto the marble floor. Oddly, he felt no compunction. This thing of indescribable evil—this was not his father. His father had died years ago. Hali had been right about the existence of the soul.

"Let me show you something," the senator said, pressing a door slide built into the desk.

The door began to open. Nick turned, drawing the nerve gun from under his waistband. Although it was too dark to distinguish the man's features, something about the figure silhouetted in the doorway made Nick's skin crawl.

"Come in, Nicholas," the senator said.

He entered the room and faced Nick, and it was as though Nick were regarding himself in a mirror: the same tall, rangy body; the same muscular limbs; identical black hair, thick and unruly; identical face, broad and handsome. Yet instead of Nick's sweet, lopsided smile, this double wore a look of unmitigated hatred, a hatred so strong it seemed to seep from his pores like a fetid perfume.

The hand in which Nick held the nerve gun began to shake.

"Your donor double," the senator said.

Was it possible? Could they have crept into the cryogenic vaults and awakened him, he who had been cloned from the same egg as Nick, who had been intended to exist solely as a donor of spare parts, a second, a replacement, a sleeper in the shadow world while Nick walked in the sunlight? (No wonder the hatred and jealousy burned so intensely in his black, black eyes.) There was one way to be certain: the three middle fingers of Nick's left hand had been crushed playing rocket polo; the replacements had come from his donor double. As if reading his mind, the other man held up his left hand and then there was no doubt; a thumb, a pinky, three stumps in between.

"I'll take those fingers back from you," the other Nicholas said. "They're rightfully mine." His voice too was identical.

"It's not my fault," Nick protested, pointing at the senator. "He's the one who cloned you and put you in storage."

But the hatred in the other Nicholas' eyes was beyond the reach of reason, wild and obsessional.

"He'll be taking your place," the senator explained. "He will admit that Hali Hasannah confused him with her psi

powers, and beg forgiveness. He will explain how the Alta-
Tyberians sent her to murder our Lifestylers and betray our
friendship and trust."

"If he's been asleep since he was born," Nick said, "then
how did he learn to talk?"

"We gave him a dose of your memory RNA"—a sample
was kept on file from every employee of Mutagen, so replacements could be easily trained in case of a death—"and inten-
sive hypnotherapy. In a few days we've taught him almost as
much as you've learned in your twenty-eight years. He's
nearly identical to you; only your closest friends will notice
the difference, and they will be persuaded to keep quiet. You
must forgive me, Nicholas, for doing this, but now that
you've seen what the Lifestylers saw, you cannot be allowed
to live. Nothing must interfere with the election of Johnny
Quog."

"You're going to kill me?" Nick asked in disbelief. It all
seemed somehow absurd and dreamlike.

"No," Senator Harmon replied, "he is."

Nick faced his double and saw that he too held a nerve
gun in his right hand. They faced each other in identical
stances—with one difference: one Nicholas' hand shook while
the other's was steady as the earth.

The other Nicholas smiled. "We're more than twins. I
know every thought you're thinking. You can try to run from
me, but I'll know where you're hiding. You can try to trick
me, but I'll know what you're planning. I'll kill you, Nick—
I'll kill you because I have one big advantage. I despise you
with every cell in my body. And I know that you couldn't kill
me if you wanted to. Go ahead." He smirked. "Try to kill
me."

Nick pulled at the trigger. His hand shook more and more.
Finally he threw the gun in the other man's face and dashing
around him, made for the door.

The senator tried to trap him by tripping the door slide on
the desk, but Nick squeezed through and raced down the
hall.

A bell was clanging—the burglar alarm. In seconds the
guards would be after him. Reaching the window through
which he had entered, Nick inched out onto the arch and,
dangling from his hands, dropped the twelve feet to the lawn.

He had hoped for a few minutes' grace, but the guards

were already out; they converged on the house from every corner of the lawn. Nick ducked behind a thick hedge of creeberry bushes and crouched there motionless, waiting for them to pass.

A voice identical to his own cried out: "Look behind the creeberry bushes."

Of course the other Nick knew about it; this was where he had always hidden as a child. In the future he would have to be more careful, he would have to double-think every move. Keeping low and weaving, Nick ran for the cover of the baroque fountain in the middle of the lawn; then he made for the street.

"There he goes," somebody shouted.

He heard footsteps running after him, shouts to stop or they'd shoot, then the insectile hum of nerve guns.

He had almost reached the slidewalk when he felt a sting in his left shoulder. His arm turned numb down to the finger-tips and swung lifelessly from the shoulder joint like some cumbersome piece of luggage. He pulled it to his side with the other hand and leaped to the express band of the slide-walk.

Since he had skipped the accelerating band, the sudden motion of the ground beneath him knocked him off his feet —yet it also sped him away from his pursuers. He lay on the plastic tread of the slidewalk for a few seconds, catching his breath, digesting the fact that his arm had been numbed. The nerve gun fired a beam of amplitude-modulated microwaves which blocked off nerve impulses for several hours. Limbs were paralyzed only temporarily, but a strike to the head was rewarded with a permanent sort of semi-consciousness called a brain-wipe.

Far behind him Nick saw his double leap to the slidewalk and race toward him. Hurriedly he rose and ran too, but the arm put him off balance and slowed him down. Fortunately the slidewalk was crowded with pedestrians, couples coming home from late dinners, teenagers out for some excitement; the other Nick dared not shoot.

As he neared the center of town the slidewalk grew more crowded and running more difficult. Noticing a free MagLev cab parked at an intersection, Nick skipped off the walk and bolted into the back seat.

"Mutagen," he told the cabby.

He had only the vaguest contours of a plan in mind, but

during the fifteen-minute trip to the labs he hoped to define it more precisely. Summoning all his remaining rationality from the haze of fear which was rapidly obscuring it, he attempted to calculate the odds.

How well were Nick I and Nick II matched?

Physically and mentally they seemed to be identical, although real-life experience must have benefited Nick I more than hypnotherapy and memory RNA could his double. Firsthand experience was always superior to secondhand, no matter how vivid the latter. Even if Nick I's reflexes were only a shade faster, his psychological insights a hair finer, that might make the difference.

Nick I's advantage.

Nick II had a weapon. Nick I had none—and even if he had, he wouldn't have been able to use it. He still felt guilty about the rat he had brain-wiped in Scolpes' lab, and killing Nick II would be like committing suicide. Killing *anyone* was like committing suicide, since it was destroying part of the total life of the universe of which everyone was a part. Yet sometimes killing could not be avoided.

Nick II's advantage.

The last time Nick had been tapped for memory RNA was nearly two years ago; he had gone through many changes since then. If the cells in the body were replaced in entirety every seven years, then he was nearly a third new, a third unknown to his dark double. Any changes in the world around him during that time would be likewise unknown.

Possibly Nick I's advantage.

The situation was not as hopeless as it had at first seemed. Two things were clear: he would need someone to murder Nick II for him, and it would have to be someone Nick had known for less than two years. Miraculously, someone came to mind. Not someone, really, but something.

They were approaching the mushroom-shaped buildings of Mutagen. Nick craned his neck to see how closely he was being followed and was startled by the presence of the other Nicholas in a cab almost alongside them, squinting along the barrel of a nerve gun aimed dead at the space between Nick's eyes.

"Get your head down," Nick shouted at the cabby, knowing that glass was no shielding for microwaves. He crouched as an insect sound passed inches from his ear.

"What's going on?" the cabby croaked.

"They're shooting nerve guns."

"Wouldn't you know it? My last fare of the day."

"Run the East Gate," Nick said.

"They'll arrest me. I'll lost my license."

Nick reached over the seat and grabbed the cabby by his collar and shook him. "Run the goddam gate!"

"Let go," the cabby grumbled, and, "Okay, okay."

The East Gate was reserved for the general public; during the day the area teemed with tourists shopping at the visitors' kiosks, strolling through the gardens and the zoo. At this hour of the night it was deserted except for a stray dog chewing on a food wrapper. The cabby swerved to avoid the animal, then lurched to the left fork of the road at Nick's command. The rarely used wheels, which the cabby had lowered to negotiate the slower speeds and sharper turns, squealed objections.

Now they descended into a shallow valley and everything vanished beneath a blanket of mist, hot and dank, generated by a powerful weather machine.

"Stop here," Nick said. He tossed a twenty into the front seat and tumbled out the door.

Fifty feet behind them the headlights of a second cab carved white tunnels in the mist. Nick climbed the shoulder of the road, leaped over the slidewalk and skittered down the wall of the ravine just as the other Nick was leaving his cab.

This particular exhibit had been conceived fourteen months ago, and the actual building of it had not been completed for almost a year. The other Nicholas couldn't possibly know where he was or what lay in store for him. The mist obscured the contours of the late Cretaceous landscape, the darkness hid the sign which said: "PLEASE DO NOT LEAVE THE SLIDEWALK—THIS ANIMAL IS DANGEROUS!"

Nick began scaling the opposite wall of the ravine. It would have been difficult enough with two arms; with one arm the task was torturous. Furthermore, humidity had turned the wall to mud; ledges crumbled beneath his weight. He tried to climb silently, but his breath was rasping, and rocks, dislodged by his feet, rained over the ground. He was nearing the top when the flashlight beacon picked him out. With a last burst of strength he scurried the last few feet; he had succeeded in pulling most of his body over the top when he felt the microwaves hit his right knee.

Now all he could do was crawl like an animal, drag himself with right leg and left arm through the mud until he reached the swamp—the foul-smelling oatmeal slime from where, so many millennia ago, life had first crept—and lay there listening to the wild percussion of his heart.

"I'm coming for you!" the other Nicholas shouted.

Nick chuckled softly—he dared not make too much noise for fear of rousing the assassin prematurely. No, he and his twin were nothing alike. The other Nicholas was himself of two years ago, conceited, brash and foolish; he had never fallen in love with an alien woman or been hunted by the police, he had never climbed through a transdimensional window and learned the weaknesses of the Lifestylers. A strange peace crept over him as he lay there listening to the other Nicholas following in his footsteps, skittering to the bottom of the ravine and climbing the opposite wall, huffing and puffing as he pulled himself over the top. Even if he were to die that night, Nick thought, he would have no regrets about his life. How many men could say the same?

"Come on out!" the other Nicholas shouted. "Come out now and I'll make a clean kill. Otherwise you'll pay for wasting my time."

That's right, Nick thought, shout. Make all the noise you can. My friend is a heavy sleeper.

"Know what I'll do when I find you? Carve off those three fingers you took from me and get somebody to sew them back on. . . . Come out, damn you!"

From where Nick lay, he could see the beam of the flashlight penetrating the mist. The slime had soaked into his clothes and, despite the heat, he felt a chill.

"I'll live! I'll live and you'll die because I've got *hate*! I've got a pound of hate for every day that I slept while you laughed and danced and made love. Love's weakened you, Nick, but hate's made me strong!"

The voice was close now and coming closer. Nick could see his feet sinking into the swamp only ten feet away. The flashlight beam swept the ground and Nick pulled his limp arm away just in time.

"*Show yourself, you fucking coward*," he screamed, and that scream did it.

The Nick who held the nerve gun whispered, "Holy shit . . ." as the tyrannosaurus rex reared over him. It seized him around the waist with a three-fingered claw and lifted him like a rag doll, twenty feet to its mouth. The scream was hideous; it ceased suddenly with a snap of teeth and a grinding of bone. Blood sprinkled Nick like an afternoon shower. He rolled onto his back and looked up, and against the sky he could see a pair of legs dangling from the enormous mouth.

He lay very still for the next two hours. Then, moving softly so as not to reawaken the monster, he started for the ravine. The life had come back to his arm and his leg was prickling with sensation.

✷ II ✷

"You changed," Senator Harmon said as Nick entered the study.

"It was a little messy. I got his blood on my clothes so I went back to his apartment and took a clean pair of tights." He smiled. "We're the same size, you know."

"Did anybody see you kill him?"

Nick shook his head. "He was riding in a cab. I pulled up alongside and shot him through the window."

"And you're positive you hit him?"

"Right between the eyes."

The senator seemed satisfied. "*You* are my real son, Nicholas. You will be a credit to me in the Peace Party. If you carry out your denunciation of the alien as well as you have my son's murder, I will see to it that Johnny Quog appoints you to an important post."

"I'm afraid not," Nick said, coming closer.

"Of course, if you would prefer to stay at Mutagen I can arrange for you to be promoted to section director, or transferred to—"

"No, what I mean is, Johnny Quog won't be appointing anyone to important positions. Johnny Quog's going to withdraw from the election."

"I see no chance of that."

"Oh, I do. Very definitely. And you won't be arranging any promotions either."

"And why not?"

"Because of your death."

Nick pulled at one of the servicing tubes. It gave way easily and the milky fluorocarbons began spilling onto the floor.

"What are you doing?" Replace that tube immediately. . . ."

Of course it was a projection on his part—the dull eyes bulging from their parchment sockets could not show terror, yet Nick imagined they did.

He pulled loose a second tube, and a third. One poured a brackish bile, the other a clear fluid, and all three ran together on the marble floor, swirling prettily, like the patterns on Indian endpapers.

"You fool!" the speaker crackled. "Put them back! Put them back!"

From the corner of his eye Nick saw a flash of light, like the glint of an emerald. The light defined a disembodied hand, a ghostly green hand which began lifting the tubes from the floor and fitting them back on the metal nipples. Only a psych field amp could produce such a limb, but where could the machine be? Built into the desk? No—it must have been built right into the senator's jar, interfaced directly with his brain.

He pulled at the green hand, and the solidity of it was startling, the cold lifeless surface smooth as plastic, composed of pure thought electronically amplified. He pulled harder, again disconnecting the tube, and suddenly the hand turned and leaped at him like some savage animal. The fingers closed around his neck and he felt the walls of his trachea collapsing, the blood welling in his head, the dizziness, the red behind his eyes. *No*, his thoughts screamed, *it cannot end like this, not when I have come so close. . . .*

A white-hot point of concentration formed within his throbbing brow. Moved by some force finer than consciousness, it passed outside his head and drifted to the floor directly beneath the life-preserver jar. Then it swelled into a transdimensional window. Nick retained awareness just long enough to see the huge jar containing the senator plummet down the hole, down into the chill grayness, the endless grayness; then he blacked out.

PART VIII
Epilogue

Nick and Hali sat on the lawn outside Post 51 while small clouds raced overhead, casting fleeting shadows across the warm, bright sun. She watched, amused, as he pulled a blade of grass and, stretching it between the thumbs of his cupped hands, blew a honking sound from it like the cry of a goose.

"You are a man of many talents," she said. "Rocket polo expert, lover, savior of the Federation—and now I see you are also a musician."

Nick bowed modestly.

"Again yesterday," she continued, "Morgan Grim visited me to apologize. He told me how proud the company was of you, and that they had arranged a special training program so that you could become a genetic engineer."

"Not really an engineer," Nick explained, "just a glorified lab technician. But it's a lot more interesting than public relations, and I get to work with Doc Scolpes."

"I am so happy for you."

They smiled politely at each other, each striving to avoid the potential misery the day held in store; after all, what had to be had to be, and why suffer it unduly?

A few minutes later Scolpes emerged from the post and waddled across the lawn in their direction. He still wore his sterile suit, having only had time to remove the cumbersome helmet. Cradled in his arms was the cryogenic briefcase Hali had brought to the planet long weeks ago.

They rose to greet him. He held the briefcase while Hali snapped the handcuff, chaining it to her wrist.

"I believe these corrected polynucleotides will ensure many generations of happy, healthy Alta-Tyberian infants."

For a minute Nick could almost see Scolpes as the grandfather, bouncing thousands of almond-eyed, blue-beaked cherubs on his knee.

"We cannot thank you enough," Hali said. "May there always be an exchange of love and knowledge between our people."

Scolpes bowed as well as he could with his belly in the

151

way, and kissed her long, delicate hand. Then, warning Nick
to be back at the lab in an hour to assist with an experiment,
he left them.

"Your luggage is waiting in the cab," Nick said.

"Well then, let us be going."

They rode in silence, Nick staring out the window. He saw
her sitting on board a great silver ship, crossing the oceans of
galaxy at near-relativistic speeds. Time would pass more
slowly for her; when she arrived on Alta-Tyberia she would
be only months older, while Nick would be an old man. To
all the other barriers separating them would be added the distance of age.

As they were nearing the spaceport, the newsman on the
radio announced that by order of a special emergency act of
congress, presidential elections were being postponed for six
months while the Peace Party convened to choose a new candidate. The right wing of the Peace Party, from whose ranks
Johnny Quog had been drawn, had been completely discred-
ited by the damning accusations of the Lifestylers, the suspi-
cious disappearance of Senator Harry Harmon, and Johnny
Quog's nervous breakdown during the inquiries that followed.
Presumably the new candidate would be offered by the left
wing of the Peace Party, an independent group with strongly
populist leanings.

They arrived at the terminal twenty minutes early. Nick
bought her an armful of magasettes and microfiches.

"I see," she said, "that I will not be at a loss for reading
matter."

"Hali . . ." he said.

"Don't."

"Hali, please, stay here with me."

Suddenly she was angry. "Why must we go through this
again? Haven't we made ourselves miserable enough? It cannot be, Nick Harmon, it simply cannot be! I was sent to your
planet with these samples"—she patted the briefcase—"and I
must return with the antidote."

"You could ship the briefcase alone," Nick suggested for
probably the thirtieth time. He already knew the answer but
he couldn't help himself.

"No, I could not! It is my duty to see it safely back to
Alta-Tyberia. All my life I have been trained for this one
task. If I did not complete it properly, I would have no regard for myself. You could not love such a person."

"Yes I could," he said, even though he knew she was right.

The announcement of the shuttle boarding came over the loudspeaker. She stood up, straightening her dress.

"Goodbye," she said, as formally as if they'd just met.

"Goodbye," Nick said. "Maybe I'll see you again some . . ." The words caught in his throat. No longer able to control the need welling within him, he kissed her and held her very tight.

She whispered in his ear, "I will never forget you, Nicholas Harmon."

Then she was walking to the gate, and then she was passing through the boarding arch, stopping to wave, and then she was no more.

He could feel the shuttle lift off from where he stood—the floor literally shook—and the waterfall roar of the rockets penetrated even the soundproofed walls of the terminal. Finally he walked to the window and watched the shuttle, a blazing point, being swallowed up by the sky.